Paperback: 978-1-923184-23-7

Ebook: 978-1-923184-22-0

A COZY SAPPHIC PARANORMAL ROM-COM

ALI K. MULFORD & K. ELLE MORRISON

*Dedicated to all the hot girls
who drink cold brew ;)*

DEAR READER,

Though this cozy romance is light hearted and full of all the fall feels, we'd like to remind you to protect your mental health. Topics within this book include violence, death, monsters and other supernatural beings, alcohol, and sexually explicit scenes between two consenting adults.

To LAKE NEVERMORE
MAPLE HOLLOW
HAUNTED WOODS
SWAMP
TRATTORIA OCCULTO
WITCHES HAT
LIBRARY
GRAVEYARD
WISHING WELL
TOWN HALL
POLICE MEDICAL
MIDNIGHT MARKET
PUMPKIN PATCH
Antiques
CINEMA
WHAT WE DO IN THE SH
PRACTICAL MAGIC
BREAKING DAW

N
W
E
S
BATS & BROOMSTICKS B&B
FULL MOON BAKERY
GHOULISH ANTIQUES
STARS AND STONES
TCH'S BREW
Black Cat Knit Shop
POISON APPLE APOTHECARY
TO SUGAR PLUM VALLEY
DRY CLEANER & LAUNDROMAT
BLOODY MARY'S
Luna's Hairdresser
POST OFFICE
Broomsticks
mes & Tomes
CAULDRON CANDLE SHOP
BOOKS
PALM READINGS
BISHOP'S ORCHARD

1
RAMONA

The old man had finally croaked.

At last, it was time to collect his despicable soul.

I had to give Saul his due for making it this long. At the ripe old age of eighty-seven, he'd committed plenty of sins worth an eternity of the most delicious punishments. The boss would be pleased.

I fixed my cufflinks while I strode down the picturesque Harvest Grove Drive to No. 38. With a tune on my lips, I walked straight through the old man's triple-locked front door and into his disorderly living room. The wealth and status for which he'd so willingly traded his soul had been squandered ages ago. Where there should have been mourners or flowers, there were only cockroaches and empty takeout containers.

"Saul Henderson," I purred, folding my arms with a pleased smirk. "Your time on this plane is up. You're mine now."

I moved closer, and something soft shifted under my

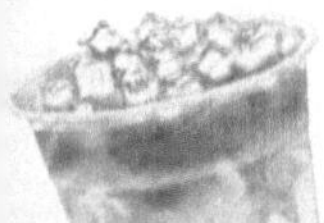

Gucci loafer. I glanced down to find a thin line of yarrow and salt that created a ring around the recliner that had become Saul's deathbed. My brow perked. The cloying scent of herbs wafted from a bowl that sat next to the chair, accompanied by a hunk of freshly forged iron and a black tourmaline crystal.

"Well, that's a new one. Trying to ward against me, old man?" I mused when my eyes met his open, unseeing ones. "Your witchy bullshit won't keep me from my collection."

Powdered sugar still clung to the corners of his mouth. I looked around the room and spied a half-eaten box of apple cider donuts on the coffee table. I knew for a fact those weren't just any donuts, but the most coveted baked goods in all of Maple Hollow. Captain Geriatric must've been waiting in line all morning for them.

I grabbed the box and tucked it under my arm. "Waste not."

The dead often missed the sweets of the living, but there'd be none where he was going.

At least he'd died eating Eloise's famous donuts. I was rather fond of her and her brother, Wyatt, the werewolf who owned Full Moon Bakery. He knew the right salt-to-sugar ratio when it came to my favorite apple tarte tatin, but ever since his younger sister had joined his ranks, the confectionaries had become even more sinfully decadent.

I drummed my red-polished nails across the pastry box as I looked at Saul's wan face. "You don't mind, do you? They'd pair nicely with the Colombian cold brew sitting in my fridge." When Saul didn't reply—*because he'd been dead for hours*—I let out a wistful sigh. "Well, I'd love to stay and chat, wrinkles, but you know, no rest for the wicked."

Another long moment of silence. Not even a stirring in the ether.

His spirit must have been in shock to not protest my claim on it.

Nonetheless, I reached into the air between us, swirling my L'Occitane-lotioned hand as it pierced into the void and beyond, feeling for his soul, which should still be clinging to his body.

I searched and searched . . . *and searched* . . . and felt nothing.

My gut plummeted.

"What the . . . ?"

I poked at the air with more force, grasping for what was rightfully mine. Focusing all of my magic, I let the tendrils of my essence stretch into the far reaches of oblivion, but in the end, I came back with nothing.

"Where the fuck is your soul?" My eyes widened in fury at the limp sack of stale blood and human flesh.

It was all coming together now. The crystal, the herbs, the iron . . . the odd expression on Saul's mottled face. Someone had beat me to the jump. Someone had taken what was *mine.*

There would be literal hell to pay for this theft.

Still holding the box of donuts, I leaned forward and pulled the collar of Saul's shirt toward his shoulder.

"Shit!"

The sigil—*my sigil*—had been broken. My mind reeled. Someone had broken a powerful demon's sigil. That kind of arcane horsepower was upper-management hell mojo. Who had the kind of magic to pull this off?

I swept a hand through the air, sensing, probing.

There were no threads of magic that I could detect, and the smell of the place was covered by the pall of incense.

The herbs burning in the bowl caught my eye again. Lavender, mugwort, and the smallest hint of wolfsbane. An odd blend, to say the least. Nothing any of the local witches would openly use with the number of werewolves they were rubbing elbows with these days.

Who would make such a bizarre concoction? My thoughts immediately flew to a certain someone, her image conjured unwillingly behind my eyelids.

If there were anyone who would have insight into the perpetrator, it would be a certain apothecary witch with fiery red hair and an attitude I loved to ignite like a spark to a mound of dry kindling. A little thrill ran through me. It had been months since I'd spoken to Iris, only catching glimpses of her in the town square or through the café window. It had delighted me that she'd been brash enough to ask for an extension on our deal—and even more that we'd sealed that addendum with a scorching kiss over the summer. My lips curled into a sharp smile even through the frustration. I had that witch on my hook, and now all I had to do was reel her in.

I picked up the bowl with my free hand, snarling as powdered sugar tipped from the donut box and onto the satin vest of my custom suit that had cost more than most people's houses.

I gave one last cursory glance over the squalid room. "This isn't over. I've never lost a soul to anyone, and I don't intend for *you* to be the first." I bid Saul's corpse a disgruntled farewell as a devious smile stretched my lips. "Time to go find my little witchling."

2
IRIS

I drummed my fingers on the gnarled wood of the apothecary desk. Once again, here I sat, bored out of my mind. I'd already bottled the most recent batch of sleep elixirs, dusted dozens of shelves—without using levitation, might I add—*and* started teaching myself an ancient summoning incantation from one of the oldest spell books that Bones and Tomes had in its archives, because all of that was better than just staring into space.

If I didn't get a reprieve soon, I might start hand-sewing bowties for Ichabod. The black cat cracked one eye open from where he slept on the floor in a circle of early autumn sunlight as if to say, *Don't you dare.*

Never had I longed for the busy season like I did now. A few tourists had filtered in to take some photos or videos for social media, but the weeks leading up to Halloween were typically slow. With the recent uptick in lifestyle influencers, we'd had our fair share of bloggers, travel enthusiasts, and nostalgia-seeking city dwellers visiting lately. The kicker was that even with the somewhat steady stream of visitors,

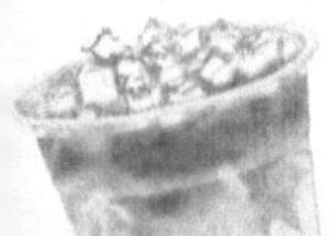

there hadn't been much more business. I knew it would pick up as we moved closer to Halloween, but I needed something to pull me out of this funk *now*.

"I could really go for some townsfolk catching a rare and mysterious stomach bug or poisoning from a bad batch of hard apple cider right about now," I mused to a half-listening Ichabod. "Or better yet, a salacious scandal where several people contract some sort of supernatural STI. That's the ticket. Drama and a brain puzzle all in one. Perfect."

When the midnight cat didn't even deign to peek at me, I sighed heavily. Everyone in Maple Hollow was far too healthy and vanilla for the coven's apothecary business these days.

With a grumble, I stared out the fogged windows and watched the leaves dance around the witch-hat gazebo at the center of town. Most of them had already changed, but some still held fast to the last bits of summer, the greens fading to vibrant yellows and oranges with burgundy and browns peeking through. A foliage hunter's dream.

Soon, our little town would be overrun. Normally, I was the poster child for the Halloween spirit, but thoughts of the Halloween Festival only brought the smallest flare of excitement . . . probably because I didn't have my best friend to enjoy it with anymore.

As if summoned by my thoughts, Jordyn stumbled through the front door, making the bells clang uproariously before she closed it behind her. She looked both shocked and frazzled by the sound, as if we didn't both have regular nightmares about phantom chiming bells after busy days.

"Sorry, sorry!" she called as she smoothed her tousled brown hair.

I eyed her swollen lips, askew cardigan, and one button

of her blouse in the wrong hole. "You couldn't keep it in your pants until the end of the workday?" I snarked, flipping through the spell book for something that would quell the libido . . . but I knew those only worked on men. There was no spell big enough to keep two hot women from banging, praise all the sapphic gods. "I know you and Harlow are sickeningly and irrevocably in love, but you'd think after a year, you would cool it a little bit."

"We got carried away." A deep red blush crept across Jordyn's nose and cheeks. She couldn't seem to wipe the shit-eating grin off her face, though. "What needs doing?"

Me, obviously, but there was a fat chance of that happening anytime soon.

"Nothing," I groused. "But stay over there and tidy the dry herbs or something. I don't need your post-carnal aroma and afterglow to dampen my already chipper mood."

Jordyn lifted the neckline of her sweater, sniffed it, then shrugged. "Slow day?"

"You could say that." I twirled a pencil between my fingers—a new trick I'd been perfecting lately. The movement attracted the true owner of the apothecary, Ichabod. His black paw swiped at my small entertainment and sent it flying across the desk. With my full attention, he headbutted into my hand, purring like a little motor.

"I really am sorry for being late. Do you need a pick-me-up? I'll watch the front while you run and grab a coffee." Jordyn's overly sweet apology made me feel worse about my attitude. It wasn't her fault I was in such a slump. I liked Harlow, and I was happy for both of them; I just couldn't help but wish that Jordyn and I were still in the same phase of life, just like we always had been until recently.

"Maybe later." I gave her a smile that hopefully said I

wasn't holding her blissful romance against her. "You know, a bunch of apples have gone missing from the orchard lately," I hedged. "We should go investigate."

"Squirrels," Jordyn answered with a flick of her wrist. "Case closed."

"Randy thinks there are people squatting in the pumpkin patch."

"Just the local ghouls."

"Oh, come on!" I urged. "Let's get the Scooby Gang back together. I'm going to die from boredom and need something stimulating! A mystery to solve or someone to save! And you're never around to hang anymore, which isn't your fault," I added hastily, "but it would be nice to have *something* to do together again."

Jordyn arched a brow at me as she rearranged the wicker baskets near the door. "I think you need to get laid."

"I've already banged all of the single witches in this town." I pouted. "The vamps don't like the taste of my witch blood, the monsters are all emotionally unavailable, and there's not a single lesbian mermaid in the swamp. Can you believe it? Mermaids, Jordyn! You'd think it'd be a sure thing! Everyone knows there's nothing gayer than freaking mermaids." I dropped my head into my hands. "I've run out of options."

"Wyatt's little sister is gay," Jordyn offered.

"Your girlfriend's sister's crush's baby sister?" I asked, pointing out the many ways that relationship would fail before it even started. "The last thing I need is to get involved in werewolf politics. They're messy as fuck. Maybe I can cast some sort of conjuring spell to find my perfect woman."

I looked down at my book, but I knew damn well that there were no love spells within its pages.

Jordyn snorted derisively. "Yeah, 'cause that has worked out so well for us in the past." With a flick of her wrist, she magically shut my book. "Slow down there, *Practical Magic.* You're going to sprain something."

I ignored her and shouted to the ceiling, arms spread wide, "Moon Goddess, send me a hot lesbian—"

And *right* at that inopportune moment, Ramona Henry walked through the door.

"Not *that* hot lesbian," I grumbled to myself.

Jordyn burst into laughter. "Gotta be more specific with those prayers, Iris," she teased as Ramona strode deeper into the apothecary. Her giggles died when Ramona gave her a cold, steely look. "Afternoon, Ramona."

Ramona replied to Jordyn's greeting with a mere purse of her lips. She gave off the same energy as the New York execs who were dragged around town by their children: cold, robotic, menacing. But beyond the expensive tailored suit and eyeliner so sharp it could cut glass, she was positively demonic. It was the way she moved and her eerie silver eyes that gave her away. She usually wore sunglasses during tourist season so no one would ask to take selfies with her, but today, her eyes were on full display and seemed to be tracking my every movement. Her raven hair was pulled back into a slick bun, not a single hair out of place. She wore shined Oxford loafers, bloodred nails, and a smudge of burgundy lipstick that demanded all of my attention. She was all angles, her features sharp and predatory as she twisted her head to look from Jordyn to me.

My mouth went dry when our gazes met. I braced my forearms on the desk. Every time Ramona made eye contact with me, my knees went weak. She was the most other-worldly and gorgeous being I'd ever met, *and* the broker holding my debt. I shouldn't want to mess with such a powerful demon, but I was drawn to her like a soul to a summoning circle.

"Can we help you with something?" I rasped, my pitch higher than my usual customer service voice.

"Yes." She glowered. "*You* can."

My stomach twisted, and I had to stop myself from leaping over the counter to answer any question she might have. Instead, I cleared my throat.

Come on, Iris! Play it cool!

Ramona dropped a white confectionary box on the desk. "Here."

I opened the top to reveal six and half apple cider donuts from Full Moon Bakery.

"Oh," I said, instantly reaching for one.

"Wait!" Jordyn called, stalling my hand as she walked over to inspect the box. "Only six left in a box that holds a dozen, and one has a giant bite taken out of it?"

Ramona shrugged. "The man I took them from won't be missing them."

Jordyn retracted her arm like one of the pastries had tried to bite her. "You gave us a dead guy's donuts?"

The corner of Ramona's mouth tipped up. "If you don't want them, don't eat them."

I snatched one of the donuts that didn't have a bite mark before Jordyn could stop me and shoved the entire thing into my mouth like a chipmunk with an acorn.

Jordyn's eyebrows shot up. "Seriously?"

I could barely speak, my mouth was so full. Luckily, my best friend was fluent in Mouthful Iris as I said, "Eloise only makes thirty boxes of these a day, and I'm never up early enough to wait in line."

Jordyn rolled her eyes before returning her attention to Ramona, who had moved to one of the herb baskets next to the checkout desk. "What are you looking for, demon?"

"This." Ramona turned her hand over, and a copper bowl of burnt herbs appeared as if she'd pulled it out of some pocket realm.

My eyes widened in awe. Her magic flowed around her as easily as she breathed. Of all the magic-wielding beings who lived in Maple Hollow, none could manipulate the forces of nature like demons could.

Jordyn took the bowl, sniffed it, then set it between the two of us. It wasn't hard to figure out that it was a mixture of common protection herbs. But there was something else that had been ground up and burned to ash at the bottom of the vessel. I dipped my finger in and brought it up to my nose.

"Well, that's interesting." I tapped the tip of my finger to my tongue and tasted the earthy mix of celery and licorice. "Angelica root."

"Someone was trying to make gin?" Ramona flipped her hand again, and the bowl disappeared.

"I doubt it." I pursed my lips, considering. "Though humans use it for alcohol, the most common use would be a psychic cloaking spell along with protection and purification."

"Why would someone use that?"

"I can't be sure, but it was known to be used in darker magic curses. It blocks out evil forces. Historically, witches used it to hide from more powerful beings when they had less-than-honorable tasks." I smiled awkwardly. "Nothing like having your wickedness interrupted to ruin a witch's night, I guess."

Ramona leaned in close, her perfume overpowering the last remains of the herbs on my tongue. My breath hitched when her finger brushed my bare arm.

"Pull yourself together," Jordyn muttered from the corner of her mouth.

I anxiously tucked a strand of hair behind my ear to put more space between us. I couldn't help it. There weren't a lot of creatures that put me on edge, but Ramona was one of them.

"So you think it's witch magic?" Ramona murmured.

Jordyn shrugged. "Could be other things. There are a few creatures that can enact curses of this kind: succubi, vampires, banshees . . . demons."

"And what about a curse that could cleave a soul from its binding?"

"Are you saying you *lost* a soul?" I asked.

Ramona's eyes found mine again. "I didn't *lose* anything," she said tightly. "A soul has been temporarily misplaced. And when I find the person who has made the fatal miscalculation that it was safe to steal from me? Let's just say it's been a long time since I've stretched those particular muscles and I'm going to have *fun* exercising them." Her eyes lingered on me, sweeping up and down my body. "I'm a bit territorial about things owed to me."

"Noted," I said thickly, knowing she spoke of the debt I owed her.

Our first kiss had sealed our deal—one I had made for information last year.

Our second one was for a two-month extension and had taken place at the witch summer camp on Lake Nevermore.

Both played on a constant loop every night before I went to sleep. There was nothing to compare them to. The hunger and possession in Ramona's electrifying kisses were a drug all their own.

And all I owed her was a date.

One simple date and then our deal would be over and I'd probably never speak to the demon again.

Every time I spied Ramona in Maple Hollow, I wondered if that would be the day she'd call in my debt. I saw it in her eyes every time she looked at me: the anticipation, the thrill of a debt unfulfilled.

I mindlessly rubbed a hand across my collarbone where her sigil branded my skin, and her eyes caught the movement. The heat around my collar intensified.

Jordyn, my constant savior and supreme clit-blocker, finally broke the tension with an awkward, "Right. Well, if we hear anything about a misguided witch running around snatching souls, we'll let you know."

Ramona nodded. "Good." She gave me a panty-dropping wink before she sauntered out of the shop.

As soon as Ramona vanished outside, Jordyn lifted her hand and sliced it through the air in front of me.

I eyed her incredulously. "What are you doing?"

"Seeing if I could cut the sexual tension."

I balked. "Ramona could have sexual tension with a freaking telephone pole."

"Not doubting that," Jordyn agreed. "But she definitely has it with you. Be careful with that one, Iris. Demons are bad news. Even *you* would be out of your depth with her."

"I know better than to mess around with a demon," I said breathlessly. "Well, more than I already have."

"You seriously need a chaperone on that date you owe her or you'll be naked before the first course."

All sorts of sinful images of me spread out over the fancy linen tablecloth flashed through my mind. Forget dinner when I could be the main course.

"Iris!" Jordyn clapped in the air in front of me as if I were Ichabod knocking potions onto the floor. "Promise me. No demon fucking. It's part of the coven bylaws for a reason. Ramona is dangerous."

Jordyn had little room to talk since her ex-girlfriend, Lou, had been part demon and they'd been together until Jordyn's—now long gone—commitment issues had gotten in the way. Lou was an exception, I knew that. She'd been more human than demon, which had deemed her docile enough in the coven's eyes. Ramona, on the other hand, was ancient, powerful, and unpredictable. "Calculated chaos" as our elders would say. Our mayor, Billy Bacchus, welcomed the demons so long as they vowed to use their powers to protect the town from humans. And so far, Ramona had kept her word. But none of that mattered to the coven.

I bit my lip, shoulders deflating. "I promise. No demon fucking."

3
RAMONA

For all its small-town charm, Maple Hollow did have one excellent bar where patrons could partake in artisanal ciders, autumnal beers, *and* deals with their friendly local demons. Customers of The Bloody Mary were safe on Wednesday nights, though. I took the night off from luring wayward souls to catch up with my closest—albeit only—friend, Naphula. My fellow demon and I liked to meet for a weekly debrief on everything from the goings-on in hell to the unsightly new logos for the Halloween Festival.

The Bloody Mary was all dark wood and sumptuously upholstered leather, giving the illusion of a Victorian gentle-man's club—though the bartender didn't appreciate it when I pointed out the anachronisms. I rapped my knuckles on the polished bar, prompting Stephanie to refill my whiskey glass. Our resident zombie, Stephanie, was the owner and head bartender. Her ghoulish grey color was a dead giveaway, but she kept herself put together enough to

convince the tourists that she was just *really* good at costume makeup.

I saluted her with my newly refreshed glass. "Thanks, babe."

"You're the only one strong enough to guzzle this jet fuel." Her ragged voice croaked with humor as she tucked the bottle away.

She was right. Even Naphula preferred more refined liquor. But on a night like this, I needed a little slice of home. Imported whiskey from hell was a fun party trick for any human daring enough to try it, but even the largest body-builder couldn't handle more than a sip before feeling the rage of hellfire climbing up their throat. Aside from a hearty laugh, a bet was just as good as a deal during a slow quarter.

"I just picked up a body in the apple orchard," Naphula said to Stephanie. "Rudy should have some fresh brains for you down at the morgue, if you're interested."

Stephanie weighed her head from side to side in contemplation, and a couple at the other end of the bar tittered as if we were putting on a live show for them. Some people really couldn't believe what was right in front of them. Why would two paid actors be stationed at a little bar on the quiet end of town? What kind of budget did they think Maple Hollow had?

Stephanie threw a bar rag over her shoulder and wandered over to freshen up their drinks, leaving Naphula and me to chat without any prying ears.

"A body in the apple orchard. Classic." I clicked my tongue and looked sideways at Naphula. "So business is good, then?"

"Slow. I'd been waiting too long for that one to kick the

bucket," she replied with a chuckle. "That's the problem with doing so many deals with the paranormal. Some of those motherfuckers don't drop for centuries."

Naphula and I had been friends since the turn of the eighteenth century and had entered into many soul-snatching competitions over the years. No one could close a deal like Naphula. Her soul count was in the tens of thousands. Almost as impressive as my own.

Naphula knocked back the rest of her martini and slid the glass across the bar right as Stephanie placed a fresh one in front of her.

"Thanks, Steph," she said, winking at the bartender's slick moves.

The opposite side of my coin in every way, Naphula's chrome-silver hair was cut in a sharp bob, and she didn't need the illusion of smoky eyeshadow to show off her obsidian eyes. She was like my photo negative, and we had the same impeccable taste in all that human luxury had to offer. It really was no wonder that we'd become fast friends when a dim-witted human had summoned both of us at a crossroads in Rome. Back then, she'd painted her lips with blood instead of Dior, but still . . . she was always the height of fashion.

Now, we'd both settled into life in the sleepy little New England town of Maple Hollow, where the deals were good and the riffraff came to us. With tourists pouring in every Halloween, we always had an ample number of souls ready to be bargained for. It was like shooting fish in a barrel. No need to compete with those corporate douchebag city demons anymore. The local demons had long since realized that they benefited from Naphula and me taking up the reins. They'd reaped the rewards of being accomplices to our deals.

"What's going on with you?" Naphula pinned me with a knowing stare. "You're more sour than usual."

Only she would've picked up on that. Most people called me stoic—unreadable, even—but Naphula knew me better than anyone. My walls were shorter around her.

I licked my back molar in contemplation. "How much do you know about Saul Henderson?"

"That fried dough cart guy?" Naphula asked incredulously. "He was such a jerk. Always treated me like an asshole for asking for cinnamon sugar *and* chocolate sauce." She rolled her midnight eyes. "He was one of yours, wasn't he?"

"Damn, you remember my clients better than I do."

She shrugged. "No one makes *that* much money from a food cart at the Halloween Festival. There had to be something demonic going on. And since he's not one of mine . . ." She studied me, her expression tightening. "What happened?"

"Well, when I went to collect, his soul was missing. Already snatched by someone. And my sigil was *broken*."

Her brow furrowed, and I could see her mind flipping through a Rolodex of unanswered questions. "How is that even possible?"

"I don't know," I muttered. "I suspect the witches. There were . . . signs of magic in his house."

She took a long sip of her martini. "You think the witches are trying to start a turf war with hell again? Those bitches are so messy."

"I don't know," I hedged. "But I intend to find out one way or another."

"Hmm." She popped the martini olive into her mouth, then downed the rest of her drink and wiped her lips. "Sorry, love. I'm about to close on a client. I've got to go."

"Already?" I looked up at the clock. Only two a.m. Usually, we stayed and talked until sunrise.

"Work waits for no one," she replied with a sigh. Now *that* I understood. "I've got this girl right where I want her, too. Selling her soul to me for internet fame, of all things." She let out a rueful laugh. "I'll give her a few viral videos for her juicy soul. See you next week?"

"Yeah. Next week," I said tightly, not wanting to admit that our weekly outings at The Bloody Mary were one of the few things keeping me from tearing my skin off at the moment.

Drool spilled from Stephanie's mouth as she wiped at the condensation rings left on the bar. A quick swipe with her bar rag and her cover was once again as clear as a crystal ball. Either that or the customers would think she was really committing to the bit.

Delightful.

Maybe a new suit would help. Or brokering another deal.

Just then, I felt the thrill of an impending death hot on the wind. It tasted like spiced cinnamon and ash on my tongue. My limbs tingled in knowing. The owner of the B&B was not long for this world, it seemed . . .

Thank fucking Lucifer.

A soul collection was exactly what I needed after this shitty day. This old lady would help keep the big boss off my ass while I figured out who'd stolen Saul's soul. The last thing I needed was for Lucifer or one of the kings of hell siccing their hounds on me . . . *again.*

I threw a stack of cash on the bar, and Stephanie let out a grunt. "Leaving so soon?"

Rolling my shoulders back, I straightened my blazer. "Work waits for no one."

4

IRIS

"There you are!" I exclaimed with relief as I crunched through the thick layer of leaves to scoop up Ichabod. He purred in my arms as I tucked him against me, his little onyx body vibrating in contentment. It wasn't like him to wander off like this, so I ran right over when Randy—the new pumpkin patch caretaker—called to let me know our little familiar was loose on his farm.

The twinkling lights and rusty lanterns of the pumpkin patch had all been turned off for the night. The shed was locked up, and the customers were long gone. Artfully displayed baskets of gourds, papery stalks of dried corn, and bales of hay still sat around the central kiosk, which had been boarded up for the night, along with all of the pumpkin-carving tools and decorations.

Next to the shed was a table with all of this week's pumpkin-carving competition winners. The designs were locked in plexiglass cages for the night, as if they were as priceless as the Crown Jewels. It wasn't uncommon for

rowdy teens to cause a little mischief—like smashing perfectly carved pumpkins.

I scratched under Ichabod's chin as I wandered over and inspected the designs. Some of the them were next level: lattice work that looked like a stained-glass window, a whole patch of miniature jack-o'-lanterns, one covered in reflective mirrors like a disco ball, and, my favorite, a Frankenstein's monster with a visage that was the true likeness of Maple Hollow's mayor, Billy Bacchus.

With an approving nod, I turned toward the path between the hedges that led back to town, cat firmly in arm.

"Thanks, Randy!" I called into the night, unsure if he was even still there.

I'd been heating up my dinner of three-day-old leftovers when he'd called. Another night holed up in the apartment, alone. Jordyn was out on a date at the swamp, and I bet she wouldn't stumble home until the wee hours of the morning, if at all. I'd been bracing for it for weeks, the conversation that Harlow was officially moving into our apartment. And even though I loved Harlow like a sister, I knew it was the end of an era. The days of Jordyn and I living as the dynamic duo above the apothecary were coming to a close. I wasn't sure I was ready for it.

The sound of a horse's whinny cut through my wayward thoughts, and a giant black steed clip-clopped through the mist. The figure with a broad torso and shoulders sitting in the saddle pulled at the bit to slow the beast to a stop. Randy's large pumpkin head sat speared on the saddle horn between the headless man's legs.

"Ah, you found him," said a deep, echoing voice that bounced around his hollow pumpkin skull. "Good."

"I did, thanks," I confirmed, holding Ichabod aloft. "I'll

be sure to keep the windows closed in the evenings. Sorry, Randy."

"He's no trouble," Randy replied. "The field mice were the only ones to mind."

Randy was the town coroner's cousin, also of the pumpkin-headed monster persuasion. They both had the body of a human and the hollowed-out head of a jack-o'-lantern, but unlike his cousin Rudy, Randy normally carried his head under the crook of his arm or affixed it to his horse, Irving. He was a true spectacle who graced many a postcard at Midnight Market.

But beyond that, Randy was fascinating and a solid choice for the job that had been left vacant last year. I argued that he would've made an excellent spy since he could place his head inconspicuously amongst a pile of pumpkins to eavesdrop.

The tourists *loved* Randy too. Most of them were convinced that a whole human hid inside a torso suit. *Can't blame them for not believing it wasn't actually his headless body.* Randy egged them on a bit as well by wearing padded shoulders in his jacket, selling the lie that kept all of us safe. Tourists couldn't know our kitschily themed town was actually full of real supernatural creatures.

"Got plans for tonight?" I asked even as Irving had started meandering away.

"Yeah." Randy's hand pulled back his sleeve and held his watch in front of his orange head. "I've got a date in a couple of hours."

"Oh."

Damn, Iris. You're so bored you're trying to hang out with Randy now?

The date part didn't surprise me. You'd think being a

headless pumpkin monster wouldn't be great for romantic pursuits, but Randy was the town's Casanova, even more than any vampire or werewolf. For one thing, he was jacked. Apparently, hefting pumpkins did wonders for his physique. And despite his echoing pumpkin head, he had a deep, raspy voice that had all of the Maple Hollow residents swooning— including his cousin's wife.

What a scandal that would be.

Hell, even I'd thought about giving his gourd a ride once or twice, and I was as straight as a zigzag. I never thought a headless pumpkin monster would be the most eligible bachelor in Maple Hollow, but here we were.

"He loves to roam," Randy said with a shrug, and it took me an embarrassing amount of time to realize he was talking about my cat, not his penis. "But we've seen a few cat-eating beasts this close to the full moon. Not everyone remembers that Ichabod is under the protection of the witches in that state."

"The pack still giving you problems?" I gave him a smirk and tried to hide the blush on my nose when he leaned down to rest his forearms on his own head.

Goddess, I need to get laid.

"If they stopped marking the back acre, I'd stop complaining about them. The smell gets picked up by the wind and pushes the deer into the patch. Bad for business."

"It is pretty strong. But the humans don't usually notice," I countered, thinking of Wyatt and his pretty, off-limits sister.

"No, but those deer are eating the flowers before they can be pollinated. Can't magic up the prettiest pumpkins in all the land if there are no pumpkins to enchant." Randy clearly took his job very seriously. Being charged with a pumpkin patch in a Halloween-themed town was like being the governor or something. "No pumpkins means unhappy visitors."

"Well, let me know if you need any wardings whipped up." Randy gave me a thumbs-up, and I kissed Ichabod's head. "Come on, you little troublemaker."

"Right, well, I better head home and get ready for my date." Randy turned Irving with a sharp grip on the reins, aiming toward the edge of the pumpkin patch.

I arched a brow. "Doesn't the caretaker get the house?" I asked, hooking a thumb at the shed behind me. I knew it had a loft bedroom. "Juniper used to sleep there."

"And risk someone snatching my head by accident?" He gave a deep, throaty chuckle. "And I'm pretty sure we have some ghouls squatting in the shed too. Don't want to disturb them. The graveyard is as comfortable as any place to sleep, and there's more grazing for Irving." He patted his horse's neck. "Would you like a ride back to the apothecary?"

"No, thanks. I got it." The offer was kind but unnecessary. I was more powerful than anything lurking between the patch and the town square.

"And tell Jordyn to stop hooking up with Harlow in the patch!" he shouted as Irving sped away. "They're worse than the teenagers on vacation."

"Okay!" I called back and then muttered under my breath, "If I ever see her."

Turning back toward the town square, I pulled Ichabod up to my chest. "Just you and me, buddy."

He purred and gave an affectionate meow.

When we reached the town square, Ichabod yowled and leaped out of my arms, dashing through the crowd toward the apothecary. He weaved between legs with ease until he darted through the gap in the shop window.

I rolled my eyes. "Or it's just me, I guess."

Following my familiar's lead, I made my way through the paranormals going about their usual business while the tourists were tucked tight in their hotel room beds. The village square was alive with late-evening energy: shopping and dining at the local restaurants, going to the hairdresser, and chatting unperturbed out in the open.

I passed Billy Bacchus outside Midnight Market arguing with the police chief, Dougall McCleighton, about town ordinances. The werewolf's gruff voice clashed with the sound of Agnes and another vampire cackling on the corner. I glimpsed Willow and Wyatt drawing the curtains of the Witch's Brew Café. They turned off the lights just as Wyatt's little sister, Eloise, carried a giant stack of apple cider donuts down the sidewalk in preparation for the morning rush. A trail of already eager patrons followed her.

Crossing the last stretch of pavement to the apothecary door, I took in a grounding breath. I was about to relegate myself to a humdrum evening when a storming shadow cut across my vision and rushed toward the alley.

I knew her from the flash of her silhouette before I even caught the glint of her raven hair and silver eyes. Her long trench coat and statuesque physique were undeniable. Those long, slim fingers balled into fists. The moonlight peeked through the clouds and landed on her like a spotlight.

"And where might you be going in such a huff?" I murmured to myself.

Before I had time to think about it, my feet were rushing in her direction.

5
IRIS

I'd promised Jordyn that I'd stay away from Ramona, and I knew better than to go running after a demon down a dark alley, but something odd was afoot—*and* I was in desperate need of some entertainment. The leftover spaghetti in my microwave could wait. Ignoring the alarm bells blaring in my brain, I made a mad dash around the building.

Slinking down the alleyway, I hoped to meet Ramona at the other end of the shadowy corridor.

I waited.

Any second now.

But there was no trace of her. I couldn't have been that fast, could I?

"I thought I heard a curious pussycat on my heels."

I jolted, whirling to find Ramona behind me. "I . . ." *I didn't think this plan through! Of course, she would hear me coming from a mile away.*

She folded her arms and arched a slender black brow at me, looking somewhere between bored and annoyed. "I'll

give you one chance to tell me why you were following me down a dark alley at night."

"Well, I–I mean, you—" I cleared my throat. "You seemed upset."

"And you thought putting yourself in the path of an upset demon was a smart idea?" She didn't look mad, just disappointed.

Why did that make this even more embarrassing? I was a powerful witch, not a foolhardy child.

"I can take care of myself," I said defensively. "I've faced bigger and badder beings than you."

Her lip curled, pulling a small dimple from her angular cheek.

Goddess, help me.

She looked cocky and predatory, like a wild cat who'd cornered a plump rabbit.

I ignored the butterflies dancing in my stomach and finally asked the question that had brought me here: "Why were you stalking menacingly through the night? Well, more menacingly than usual." I cringed with embarrassment.

"What would that information be worth to you, witchling?"

A vision of sealing my first deal with her flashed through my mind. The way she'd kissed me like I was the air she breathed . . .

Goddess, that happened almost an entire freaking year ago!

I really needed to pull myself together. I should've just turned and walked away, but I was hopeless.

"I actually thought you might need my help," I supplied. "It seemed like something was wrong."

"Perceptive," she said flatly. *I may have vastly overesti-*

mated how not *annoying she found me.* "Are you sure you only followed me to offer help?"

I hadn't noticed that she'd backed me up to the wall until her long fingers reached up to tug a rogue Ichabod whisker from the collar of my cardigan. She held it between us like an offering. When I didn't take it, she tucked it into the pocket of her blazer. "Because I think you have more than just being *helpful* on your mind."

"It's a small town. Things can get a bit . . . stale," I admitted, instantly feeling as if I had just given her information she could use against me.

"My work is not for your entertainment." Her words should have sounded harsh, but they didn't hold the bite of indignation.

"Please?" I pushed, my mind floating back to the pathetic, lukewarm spaghetti in my microwave.

Mischief lit Ramona's expression. "What is it worth to you?"

"You think I'd make another deal with you? Just to have something to do?"

"It's not my job to know what people want. Everyone thinks they know what they want when they call upon me, and they never do. My true gift is to know what people *need*. What they don't know they're desperate for."

Something in the way she emphasized the word "need" made my core tighten.

"I have everything I need," I countered. I had a coven, a good job, a home, friends, family . . .

Action and adventure weren't needs. They were hobbies, if anything.

My gaze flitted to Ramona's mouth as I thought about how much I didn't *need* her kind of amusement.

Nope. Definitely not.

Ramona's silver eyes beamed in the darkness, making me keenly aware of being the sole point of her focus. It was utterly addicting.

The things I might do to be the object of her attention . . .

I shook off that thought, not sure how far I'd go to test that theory.

"Want to find out if that's truly what your soul desires?" she asked as if reading my mind.

Inching closer, she braced her forearm on the wall behind me. Her body was so close to mine that I could make out the notes of vanilla and spice in her perfume. My skin heated as I took another deep breath of *her* in.

"I think I've made enough deals with you," I rasped.

Technically, I'd made two: I agreed to go on a date with her in exchange for information about Lou's killer last year, and this summer, she'd agreed to extend the deadline for our date in exchange for another kiss . . . and what a fucking kiss it had been.

Ramona's smile widened as if she were thinking the same thing. "Oh, you and I are just getting started, red."

I rolled my eyes. "Oh, *haha*, I have red hair. Very original nickname, you corporate hellion."

"Come on. Make a deal with me," Ramona goaded, her alluring voice like a siren's song.

My stomach somersaulted at her commanding tone. "No."

"It could be fun," she purred.

"I don't think we have the same definition of *fun*. This was a mistake."

"Maybe. But do you have any better things to do?"

A small voice in the back of my head was screaming at

me to run. Not because I thought Ramona wanted to hurt me . . . at least not out of malice. I could play it safe, go back to my empty apartment to cuddle with my cat, eat a bowl of spaghetti that was fifty percent parmesan cheese, and binge-watch *Derry Girls* again.

Or . . .

"No more deals," I declared as I fixed Ramona with a glare. "But maybe helping you would be less boring. So, you can take my help with no deal or you can leave it. What will it be?"

I could tell Ramona was battling a smirk as she pursed her lips and considered me. "Perhaps a witch on the case would help," she mused. "Not that you were all that helpful with the herbs before." She sucked her cheek. "Fine. But you stay behind me and don't make any trouble for us, got it?"

"Yes!" I squeaked instantly. "Now?"

"You asked where I was going." She stepped back, brushing the brick dust off her sleeve. "You stopped me on my way to somewhere important. Somewhere I still need to be. Are you in or not?"

"Absolutely," I said a little too eagerly. Clearing my throat, I schooled my expression. "I mean, yeah, fine. Let's go."

"Excellent." The demon flashed a toothy grin. "Into the night we go, little witch."

6

RAMONA

"Where are we going?" Iris was like a Chihuahua at my heels, having to take two steps to my one.

The bed-and-breakfast wasn't far from Poison Apple Apothecary, but I could hear her heavy breaths and wondered if it was the brisk walk or her proximity to me that had her respirations quickening. Sometimes I forgot to walk at a human pace. Once, a tourist had accused me of using some sort of "moving carpet like in *Twilight.*" Whatever the hell that meant. Billy Bacchus had reported me to the demonic council for it.

I let out a grunt of frustration as I slowed down. It was a fine line, being just paranormal enough so that the delicate humans could believe this whole town was a show.

"I have a soul to collect," I answered as I listened for Iris's breathing to steady. "Second death this week, in fact. What should've been a bountiful reaping," I added bitterly.

"Sounds like a busy week for you and Rudy," Iris said, finally catching up to me.

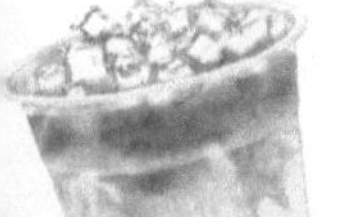

Rudy, the town medical examiner, and I had an interesting relationship, to say the least. To him, my deals were unnatural. Rich sentiment coming from a pumpkin-headed monster. But often, my job included prolonging the lives of the town residents, which made his line of work more difficult, especially when it came to the reports he had to file. Nothing a little magic couldn't fix, though. Our guy at the state department definitely knew a thing or two about deals with devils. But Rudy was stalwart about not breaking certain occult rules and believed in the cosmic order of things.

Circle of life and all that *Lion King* nonsense.

". . . and then he got his tail stuck in a bundle of rosemary."

I blinked, realizing I hadn't been paying attention to whatever Iris was blathering about.

Something about her cat, I guessed.

Her overfamiliarity rankled me. I was meant to be feared, if not revered. But a little quiet part of me was pleased that she wasn't cowed by my presence, and I let her continue nattering on about her mischievous familiar.

I relished the cool evening breeze on my skin. The colder the better, in my opinion, since my skin seemed permanently heated from the fires of hell. I should've been irked by the witch interrupting my midnight agenda, but in that moment, I couldn't seem to find the energy to care.

"Ramona?"

"Hmm?" I replied.

"Did you hear me?"

"Yes."

Iris crossed her arms in stubborn—and, if I'm being

honest with myself, adorable—indignation. "Then what was I saying?"

"Something about your cat."

Her bottom lip jutted out. "Lucky guess." As we rounded the corner, Iris's eyes fell on the Gothic abode stretching skyward in front of us. "We're going to Bats & Broomsticks?"

"The time is up for the local inn proprietor, and before her body can be disturbed, her soul must be retrieved by its rightful, new owner. Me." I could have imagined it, but I swore Iris shivered beside me.

"And how am I supposed to help with that?"

"You'll see." I opened the distance between us again, forcing her to hurry behind me.

The brick path up to the main entrance was riddled with the last fallen leaves of the year. Only enough to complement the carved pumpkins that lined the walkway up to the door. The four-story, shingled, white building was the perfect canvas for the black shutters and window boxes filled with obsidian flowers. An ornately carved sign decorated with bats and jack-o'-lanterns was mounted on the front door along with a skull-shaped brass door knocker. The residence was one of the oldest boarding houses in New England and was one of the most photographed buildings in town for its regal spires, Gothic iron fencing, and general gloom. Social media influencers loved to pose in front of the place for its spooky aesthetic.

I led Iris around to the back door that separated the guest accommodations from the family quarters. The Ketchum family had owned the place for over three hundred years, though the B&B had only been open for the last hundred.

I knew Maude's small bedroom was located on the first

floor. It gave her better access to the front when out-of-towners arrived in the middle of the night, looking to check in. Her children had moved into the rooms on the top floor when they'd become adults and had families of their own. The three other floors were every vacationer's dream.

We reached the door, and Iris narrowly missed running into me when I paused before unlocking it. "Wait here." I darted Iris a look when she opened her mouth to protest and was pleased to find that my withering stare was enough to make her close it again.

No one knew yet that Maude had finally given up the ghost, so to speak. And though Iris was a witch, she had a delicate heart, and I didn't want to risk her falling apart if there was a less-than-peaceful scene on the other side. I'd found souls in all sorts of crazy and compromising positions. My favorites were the autoerotic asphyxiations. Not that I thought old Maude was into that, but one thing I'd learned in my centuries of soul-reaping was the most vanilla-looking people were the ones you had to watch out for.

I waited until Iris nodded her head in agreement.

Good girl.

Then, harnessing my magic, I slid the deadbolt aside, cracked open the door, and stepped into the small living room. To the right was the bathroom and to the left was the main bedroom. But there wasn't a body.

As I projected out with my supernatural senses, I frowned. I should've been able to feel the soul trapped in its former meat suit, but something about this collection was off. I moved into the bedroom, fear mounting as I was met with the familiar scent of herbs.

Rushing faster, I found Maude's body serenely tucked

into her bed. Whatever had finally ended her life hadn't been a disturbance or villainous monster. Just an old woman drifting off in her sleep for the last time. I leaned in close to the bowl of herbs on her nightstand and, just as before, a hunk of iron sat next to a black tourmaline crystal. I looked down at the ring of yarrow and salt that had been broken upon the perpetrator's departure.

"Fuck." The whispered curse flew from my lips when I spied the skin above Maude's nightgown.

My sigil, which had been tattooed into her skin sixty years ago, was gone.

7
IRIS

"Alright, Detective Witchling," Ramona snarked, waving me into the bedroom at the end of the hall. "What do you see?"

Maude Ketchum, the proprietor of the Bats & Broomsticks B&B, lay serenely in her bed.

Almost too serenely.

It was as if the old lady had decided to really glam herself up for her final night on Earth. Or maybe she just donned a fancy silk nightgown and rouged her cheeks every night before bed. Who was to say? She'd been a glamorous, albeit kooky, old woman. Perfect for this town.

I folded my arms tighter across my chest as I surveyed the room, looking for any clues. There were rumors that Maude may have been part mermaid, but now that I knew she was one of Ramona's clients, the jig to her seemingly ageless appearance was up. Her daughter, Sandra, on the other hand, was part wood nymph, but those creatures aged as humans did. Now in her mid-eighties, Sandra had

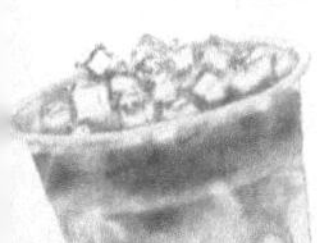

appeared older than her own mother for as long as I could remember.

"Let me guess," I muttered, bending low to inspect Maude's faint crow's feet. She still looked on the cusp of forty. "She traded her soul for beauty and youth."

"Of course she did." Ramona winked devilishly. "Too bad she didn't wish for a much longer life to go with it. Still, she made it into the triple digits. Impressive." Ramona's gaze flitted over the space. "What else do you see?"

Scrutinizing the room once more, I let out a long sigh. I'd been in this B&B many times, and aside from the aesthetic being *eclectic*, there wasn't anything particularly magical about it. The clashing Victorian wallpaper, faded tapestries, threadbare carpets, and mishmash of antiques were the epitome of cozy clutter. And I especially loved the macabre bits and bobs tucked away in every corner. I eyed the stuffed raven mounted in the corner that wore a top hat, monocle, and white bowtie. He wasn't even the strangest thing in the room, but he fit right in.

"I hope it was worth it, Maude," I murmured with a disappointed tsk.

"It doesn't matter if it was or wasn't," Ramona replied, bored. "She made her choice, enjoyed it thoroughly, and made plenty of petty enemies from the attention she garnered from her neighbors' husbands—and sons. But who are we to judge the wishes of others, hmm?"

I was once again reminded of my own deal that I'd struck with Ramona. But at least the bargain I'd made had been to help my friend. That had to give me some supernatural brownie points, right? I mean, it wasn't entirely selfless. The thought of sealing a deal with Corporate Suit Mommy over there definitely had its own personal intrigue for me, if I was being honest.

I wondered how many deals this demon had sealed with a kiss. Which I shouldn't care about at all.

As if summoned by my thoughts, Ramona took a step closer, standing so close behind me that the edge of her coat brushed against my skirt. I sucked in a sharp breath when she dropped her lips to my ear and murmured, "We didn't come here to wax poetic about aging, little witch. I asked what you see."

I shuddered at the way her warm breath tickled the shell of my ear. My eyes scanned over the scene one more time. Maude's nightgown was pulled askew, her collarbone revealing the mangled mark left behind where Ramona's sigil must've once been.

"Your sigil," I whispered, clearing my throat when I sounded too breathless. "It's broken."

"Ten points to Captain Obvious," Ramona jeered. "What *else* do you see?"

"It doesn't look like she struggled," I continued. "Whoever was here before us broke the circle after her death." My gaze darted to the bedside. "There are herbs burning again," I mused as I picked up the candle wrapped in fresh angelica and rosemary. "They're the same ones that you brought us from Saul's place the other day." I sniffed the candle, the wheels in my mind spinning faster. "But these are too fresh to be from the apothecary, which means they were recently grown . . . but only the witches in town have the capability to grow them year-round. But this . . . I don't feel familiar magic here."

Ramona stroked at the notch of her throat. I hadn't noticed before, but she wore a thin, delicate gold chain from which hung a small ruby on a pendant. I saw her thoughts spiderwebbing out as she turned over the information laid out before us.

"I don't believe this is true witch magic." Something lit her eyes, some kind of recognition, and she returned her focus to the room and to me. "But I think someone is trying to throw us off the scent, no pun intended."

My gaze snagged on one of Maude's hands, which was clenched over her chest. "What is she holding?"

"If she knew she was passing, it's probably something precious to her," Ramona commented, moving closer to the bedside. "Not long ago, I collected a soul from a pixie who wanted to take her favorite starfish to the grave with her."

"A starfish familiar. Now I've truly heard everything."

"Mortal beings are sentimental like that."

I shot Ramona a morbid glance. "You wouldn't know anything about being sentimental, would you?"

"That's not true. I enjoy my possessions just as much as the next demon."

Was that supposed to be a demon pun?

A glint of something between Maude's fingers caught my attention. I gingerly pulled at the sleeve of her nightgown, and her hand tipped open just enough for me to see the walnut-sized black tourmaline nestled in her palm.

"Do you think she was already holding it, or do you think it's like a calling card for this soul thief?" I looked up at Ramona and waited for her to say something, but judging by the expression on her face, she was at a loss for words.

"I don't know," Ramona admitted tightly.

I backed away from Maude's empty vessel and dusted my hands down my sweater. "We should go ask Citrine."

Ramona gave me a sideways look. "Who?"

"I thought you knew everyone in this town?" I taunted, but when Ramona ignored my question and simply waited, I added, "She's the witch who runs the crystal shop."

"Her name is *Citrine* and she runs a *crystal shop*?" Ramona asked incredulously. "You can't be serious."

"You just told me about starfish familiars!" I blustered. "We live in a magical gathering place for the paranormal, where we not only welcome tourists but try to convince them that we are all putting on some sort of town-wide skit every year. You're a snarky demon who holds more secrets than the mayor. I'm a witch who uses real magic to heal people. We're now investigating a *second* soul snatching. But Citrine being the name of the crystal shop owner is where you draw the line?"

Ramona pursed her lips. "Point made." Her glowing silver eyes studied me. "You've surprised me tonight."

Now it was my turn for incredulity. "What do you mean?"

"You don't seem at all unsettled by the dead body in the room."

I guffawed. "Witch, remember? Death is nothing new to me."

Ramona inclined her head, impressed. The butterflies in my stomach swarmed.

Dammit, Iris! You shouldn't want to get gold stars from a freaking demon!

Most of the time, I knew better than to bask in a demon's approval. To her, I was a passing flirtation in the eternity she spent on this plane. But a little part of me wondered how often she was amused by a mortal, let alone *surprised.*

Ramona huffed out a laugh. "You *do* tend to attract the dead, as I remember."

"I do not." I rolled my eyes. "I just don't fear it. Or much of anything, including big, bad demons in Versace."

Her brows lifted at my critique. Little did she know that I thought she was the hottest being I'd ever seen in a suit, Versace or not. "You're wearing a sweater with cartoon bats embroidered on it. Forgive me for not quaking in my loafers."

"Some of the most poisonous animals in the world are adorably colorful," I warned her, knowing I was on very thin ice. "I may look sweet and innocent, but I am a very powerful witch, not some human waif."

Ramona dragged her eyes up my body so intently that I could practically *feel* her on my most sensitive skin. "I never said you were sweet and innocent."

My mouth went dry. Her elusive playfulness was gone and the prowling monster she truly was came bubbling to the surface, but that only excited me further. I knew I was stepping into the trap she was setting, but the thrill of being caught by her shot through me like a bolt of lightning.

"You get my point," I snapped, locking my suddenly weak knees. "You should behave yourself around me. Or else."

Okay, maybe that was a little too far. Nuance, Iris!

Ramona prowled a step closer, silver eyes flaring in challenge as my stomach tightened. "I can handle myself around your kind of power. But can you handle yourself around mine?"

Holy witch tits, that was hot.

This game of cat and mouse was going to my head. Part of me was terrified to find out what falling for a demon would do to me. The other part was just crazy enough to try. Jordyn would kill me if she saw me right now.

I swallowed thickly, trying to keep my confidence in my voice as I said, "I can handle it."

Ramona grinned. "I look forward to finding out."

"Maybe we should keep our relationship strictly . . . professional." I answered an unspoken question. *Goddess, I'm such a chicken.* "For the sake of your job and, uh, my soul."

That didn't dull the glimmer of mischief in Ramona's silver eyes, but her smile tightened to one of intrigue. "Fine. You can help me, no strings attached. But just so we're clear: *I* am in charge of this investigation. You're just a helper."

"I'm the Watson to your Sherlock, got it."

Ramona rolled her eyes. "That man was insufferable."

"Which one? Robert Downey Jr. or Cumberbatch?" I couldn't imagine Ramona watching films, but who could resist a sassy British detective?

"Doyle." She turned toward the door, her words trailing behind her. "Sold his soul for fame and never did deliver the love scene I demanded. Are you coming or not, Watson?"

"What? Oh. Right. Crystal shop," I said, flustered. "It's closed at this time of night, but why don't we meet at Witch's Brew tomorrow morning and head over together?"

I followed her out to the street, closing the door gently behind me so as not to wake anyone else in the B&B.

"Or," Ramona added tightly, "we can go wake up this Citrine now and intimidate the answers out of her."

"*Or,*" I cut in, emphatically waving my arms, "we don't make enemies in town when we're trying to figure out who is snatching your paydays out from under you, and you just trust me and play nice this one time."

Ramona's jaw tightened. "Fine. We'll do it your way," she gritted out. "But I don't play nice, *ever*. You would do well to remember that."

With that, she disappeared around the corner, leaving me to walk back to the apothecary with a whole lot of questions and anticipation swelling in my chest.

8

RAMONA

I sat at the small table at the back of Witch's Brew Café, staring grumpily down at my lemon blueberry scone. When I glanced up, I found the blonde café owner, Willow, and her mullet-clad sister, Harlow, watching me from the espresso machine.

"What?" I barked, making them jolt in unison.

"Nothing!" Willow squeaked. "You enjoying the scone?" She nodded at my untouched plate.

I picked up my fork and knife like I was going to impale someone with them. "Yes."

"Great!" she said through a smile that some might have called a grimace.

"Do you want a coffee?"

"Sugar-free cold brew, no cream," I snapped.

"Okay! You got it!" The human café owner knew my usual order, but she still scrawled it onto her largest plastic cup and passed it to her nepotized barista.

"Dude, chill," Harlow muttered to her sister.

The café was always busy this time of day. The creatures

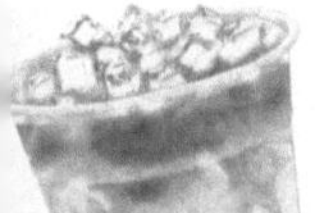

of the town filtered through the tourists and capitalized on the influx of revenue. One of the mayor's employees stood outside the café's bay windows, passing out flyers for Midnight Market, which every tourist took with a smile.

"Here you go." Harlow placed the frosty beverage in front of me, then immediately turned on her heel. She hadn't been part of the community for long, but she knew better than to linger, which meant I already liked her more than ninety percent of the locals.

At that thought, Agnes slid onto the seat beside me. *Speak of the devil.* "You're even surlier than usual," she said by way of greeting.

I lifted two fingers to my temple as I took a sip from my cup. "Agnes."

"What are you doing haunting this place so early in the morning?"

"I could ask you the same thing," I replied. "Didn't that bleach-blonde human almost *kill* you last year?"

Agnes let out a shrill laugh. "Nearly. But I've moved on." She tipped her head toward Harlow. "Her girlfriend and that redheaded witch saved me, so all is forgiven. Not to mention, they took care of Katie. Though, the new fish-monger isn't as chatty."

"Iris."

"Is that the new fishmonger's name?"

"No," I gritted out. "The redheaded witch. Her name is Iris."

"I know," Agnes said, mischievous smile broadening. "But now I know that *you* know her name, which is far more intriguing."

"Vampires," I muttered, taking another long swig of cold brew.

Her thin brows wiggled. "What a pretty penny that must have been."

Vampires were far too nosy. Agnes, in particular, was considered the town gossip, even among her band of ancient cronies. They were always watching and listening. If anyone wanted to know about someone else's business, Agnes was your gal.

I could feel her eyes assessing me, trying to find some juicy news. "It's too early for your vampire tricks."

"I thought demons loved trickery."

"Not this morning."

Agnes let out a sigh and drummed her sharp nails on the table. "We haven't seen you at the club in a while. What have you been up to?"

"Work."

"I was hoping to hear you'd found a paramour of some sort."

She was *hoping* to feed her rumor mill was more like it.

"I have had plenty of women lately, thanks, Aggie. Good thing I can magic myself clean sheets, you know?" I added with a wink, hoping the insinuation would push her to drop it.

"That's not what I meant," Agnes chastised. "Don't you ever get lonely?"

"No."

"I see I've been relegated to your monosyllabism."

I ripped a bite off my scone as if I were tearing flesh from bone. "Don't you have some vampires to mother or something?" I snapped. "I'm fine. I don't need your concern."

"Who said I was concerned about you?" Agnes balked. "If you're going to be so huffy, you can enjoy your very early morning in silence." She held up her mug, and at the silent command, Harlow rushed over to refill it. The human watched Agnes with rapt attention as the vampire took the first sip. Even after a year, Harlow was still concerned she might poison the old vampire again.

When Harlow determined that Agnes was safe, she rounded to the other tables with a pot of drip coffee and a pot of hot water. Left alone again with Agnes, I became highly aware that my morning was going to be far from silent.

"So what's new?" Agnes asked.

I looked at my watch. "Managed to give me the silent treatment for one whole minute. Good job, Aggie."

She ignored me. "Anything interesting going on in hell?"

"Nothing that would concern an immortal like yourself," I replied tightly. "But the weather is nice this time of year. Thin veil and all that." I felt a twinge of guilt for giving Agnes the ice queen treatment—not that the vampire couldn't handle it. She was a curmudgeon at the best of times, much like me.

The bell above the café door rang, and I looked up to see Iris wandering in. Her eyes panned the crowd, searching for . . . me.

I had to stifle a grin of pleasure at that fact.

She wore a wool skirt with a cream turtleneck, which would have been enough to make her look like she had stepped out of a fall-time romantic comedy, but the festive sweater vest with argyle and pumpkins across the chest solidified that she belonged in Maple Hollow. I wondered if she'd dressed extra kitschy just to spite me.

Several patrons turned to look at Iris, and honestly, who could blame them?

I let out a little grumble at myself. I didn't do sunshine

and sweetness. I was a creature of the night. Still, a small thrill zipped through me when her eyes finally landed on mine and she smiled.

What I would give to bottle up the feeling of when Iris smiled at me.

"What was that?" Agnes quipped, noticing our silent exchange. "Oh, she's coming over. So you really *do* know this redheaded witch."

"Yes. We are acquainted," I gritted out as Iris bridged the distance between us. "And I don't know her the way you're implying. She's just helping me with . . . a quandary I've encountered."

"Hey!" Iris breezed over with the easy warmth of sunlight on a cold autumn day. "Ready to go to the crystal shop?"

"You're going crystal shopping?" Agnes balked. "With Halloween Barbie over here?"

"Shut it, Aggie."

When Agnes's smile only widened, I was suddenly very aware of the fact that the vampire had wanted to see if I would come to Iris's defense.

And I'd fallen for the bait.

"We have some business to take care of with the witch who owns the shop," I said tightly.

"Soul-snatching business?" Agnes shot back.

"What do you know about that?"

"Naphula may have shared your frustrations with me," she replied with a shrug. "But you're barking up the wrong tree, I fear. No Maple Hollow witch would be stupid enough to make a deal with a demon. Though, we could use some new entertainment around here."

"No?" I arched a brow as I turned to Iris. "No witch would be foolish enough to make a deal with me, eh, Iris?"

"Nope," she rasped.

I patted my lips with my napkin, tossed it onto my plate, then rose to stand. "I'll catch you around, Agnes." I clapped her on the shoulder. "Steer clear of the nutmeg."

"That was one time!" I heard Harlow mutter as she passed by with two porcelain mugs in hand.

I snickered, not waiting to hear Agnes's farewell as I walked out the back door of the café and into the alley. I didn't look to see if Iris followed, but judging from the clopping of her high-heeled boots, she was close behind.

"So I was thinking . . . ," Iris began. I rolled my eyes and hastened my gait. "Maybe you should stay outside while I talk to Citrine. She's kind of shy and you're—"

"I'm what?" I whirled around faster than Iris could anticipate, and she collided with my chest.

She staggered back a step to catch herself, a scintillating shade of crimson coloring her cheeks. "Um, intimidating?"

"Good."

Iris cleared her throat and moved around me, giving me a wide berth. "Just let me handle it," she pushed. "Please?"

I shrugged. "Be my guest, Halloween Barbie."

"Please don't let that turn into my thing," she grumbled as she took the lead.

I slowed my pace so she could storm off ahead of me . . . and I didn't mind in the slightest that I got to watch the way her hips made that skirt swish.

Seven Hells.

9
IRIS

Ramona wrinkled her nose as we walked through the door of the crystal shop. "Why does it look like an acid trip in here?"

"It's not that bad," I murmured under my breath. I turned to take in the place, expression deflating. "Okay, maybe it's a little on the psychedelic side."

"A little? How do *you* know what an acid trip is like?"

I suddenly realized that I was several steps ahead of her because she'd paused just under the wind chimes at the entrance. Looking completely out of place amongst the glittering stones, smoke from the incense, and colorful tapestries hanging from the ceiling, Ramona grimaced at the interior.

Gripping her upper arm, I pulled her to me and escorted her to the front desk. "Tighten up your millennial grey trousers and get your head in the game, demon."

"These are slate grey and cost more than all these dusty rocks," she countered but permitted me to drag her along, nevertheless.

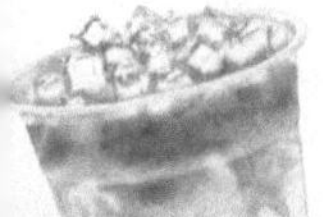

The shop was narrow and deep, aglow with salt lamps and astral projection lights that made the ceiling a swirling galaxy of purple and gold. Rows upon rows of baskets lined the walls, and a central table displayed different necklaces and rings along with delicately carved figurines in everything from agate to lapis lazuli.

"Be with you in one sec!" a soft, feminine voice called from deep within the shop.

We perused the piles of crystals while working our way toward the source of commotion. The building was enchanted to be larger on the inside, like a pocket between veils. It felt as if we'd been walking for several minutes before we stumbled upon Citrine, who was packaging up a bundle of beaded bracelets for a family in matching North Face fleeces.

A small child clung to their mother's leg and peered up at me, then homed in on Ramona, who gave the kid an empty-eyed half smile. A split second of fear strained their little face, but then they beamed up at her. I'd seen this effect before. When children came into contact with Ramona, they recognized that they weren't in danger. Adults, on the other hand . . . Well, let's just say the smart ones knew to fear her.

The kid's father turned and smiled at me. But then he spotted Ramona. "Oh, excuse us." He quickly nudged his wife and child out of our way as fast as he could.

Ramona raised her chin as they passed, assessing.

I wondered if this was how she found her targets. Did this man have debts too deep to claw his way out of without some help from hell?

I didn't need my tarot deck for a scenario to appear before me: the man losing his job in the big city and taking his family on one last vacation before uprooting their lives for another job on the West Coast. It was part intuition, part taking in his finance-bro-chic attire.

The family skittered away before I could read any more into it.

"*That* is the witch?" Ramona asked in a low voice, bringing my attention back to Citrine, who was toying with some obsidian. "She doesn't look like she could bend the forces of nature, let alone *my* sigil."

I peeked up at Citrine. She had mousy, shoulder-length brown hair, wire-rim glasses that were too big for her heart-shaped face, and brown doe eyes. She wore flowing linen clothes in burnt orange and looked like a walking jewelry display with so many necklaces, bracelets, and rings that they must add another twenty pounds to her tiny frame. A gold nose ring and stacked gold hoop earrings completed her artsy, hippie style.

"How well do you know this witch?" Ramona murmured. "She doesn't look like she can keep a secret."

I liked the way she implied that I was worthy of keeping her secrets, but I wasn't about to comment on that. "She was a few years older than me at school," I replied quietly. "And she was my camp counselor one year, but that's probably the closest we ever were. So I know a little bit about her."

Ramona guffawed, drawing the attention of a mustachioed patron perusing the labradorite. She gave the man a death glare, and he quickly butted back out of our conversation. I repressed a snicker at his terror but was starting to enjoy Ramona's effect on mortals.

"I forgot about your little witchy summer camp," Ramona said with a smirk that lit me on fire. I knew she hadn't forgotten about it. Not after the kiss we'd shared beneath the midnight trees. "So you two bonded over acoustic singing and s'mores?"

I shrugged. "She's mostly a friendly acquaintance, but she's a good person. We can trust her. I have a feeling she'd tell us whatever she knows."

"I bet I have better ways to make the little mouse squeak."

That shouldn't have been hot, but it absolutely was.

"Listen, be careful," I warned. "Citrine is a powerful witch, even more powerful than me." Ramona shot me a look. "I am powerful!" I stomped my foot indignantly, which only made her smile widen.

"Sure you are, cupcake."

"I'm serious," I whisper-hissed. "I feel bad for her, honestly. She nearly killed her last boyfriend."

"Boyfriend? She's a witch who works in a crystal shop and she's straight?"

"Not that it's any of your business, but she's pansexual."

"Interesting." Ramona shot me a look. "How did she almost kill him?"

"I don't know all the salacious details, but the coven elders said her magic nearly consumed him when they were in bed together."

Ramona let out a low whistle. "Talk about a magic pussy."

My cheeks heated. "It's the amount of her power that's the problem, not magical sex organs," I muttered. "It's a terrible curse to be that powerful." I was pushing the issue more than it needed to be. "She can never let someone in, never have a partner."

"Maybe she just needs more than one," Ramona offered,

her lips curling with mischief as she drank Citrine in. "I'm sure the right quartet of lovers would do her some good."

"What does that even mean?" I hissed. "Are you . . . into her?"

Ramona's quicksilver eyes snapped to mine as if magnetized. "Would it bother you if I was?"

"No," I said too quickly, choking on the insinuation. "It doesn't matter to me whose bed you slither into."

"Liar," she purred. She reached out and touched a strand of my hair before brushing a finger across my cheek. "Malice looks good on you, little witchling. Jealousy's the color of your eyes."

When said eyes dropped to my lips, I only had one thought: *I am so fucked.*

She pulled her hand away, leaving the ghost of her touch on my skin. I took a step back, hoping the regained ground would strengthen my trembling legs.

Thankfully, the moment was saved by Citrine calling out, "Hey, Iris!" Then adding with less enthusiasm, "Ramona. What can I do for you?"

Ramona seemed perplexed that Citrine knew her name, and the feigned humility made me roll my eyes. Ramona and Naphula were the local demons. Everyone knew who they were. Whether the two hellions thought they were more inconspicuous than they actually were or if they just expected everyone to go along with their charade, I didn't know.

"Is this a crystal dildo?" Ramona pointed to an alarmingly phallic-shaped Dalmatian Jasper.

Citrine gripped the base of the largest . . . pumpkin?

The piece had five carved pumpkins stacked on top of one another ending with a smooth nub at the very tip.

"Here at Stars and Stones, we encourage all aspects of self-discovery through certain healing crystals. The ones marked with a heart sticker are safe for internal use. This one invokes joy, loyalty, and play. It's one of our most popular items."

"Uh, right." Ramona took another long look at the crystal item as Citrine set it back down.

"So, um, yeah," I said, taking the lead in the conversation we were here to have. "I've been doing some research lately and—"

"My fellow spell nerd," Citrine said with a smile. "You've always been so clever."

Ramona stepped possessively into me at the fondness in Citrine's voice. The butterflies in my stomach danced anew at the subtle movement.

"I wish I could work spell magic as skillfully as you do," I replied, placing an affectionate hand on her arm.

Ramona stiffened next to me.

Okay, maybe I was making her squirm as a small act of revenge, but she deserved a taste of her own medicine. Sue me!

"Actually," I continued, "I'm looking into curses that require crystals and herbs, specifically angelica root, iron, and black tourmaline."

Citrine pursed her lips. "Those aren't unusual ingredients for protection." She stared at the ceiling contemplatively. "More common in run-of-the-mill spells than actual curses. But protection spells could be used to cloak a curse, I suppose. If the magic wielder were being extra careful."

It looked as if Citrine were trying to work out a riddle. I could tell she was flipping through the stacks of information she'd locked away in her big brain.

"Anything powerful enough to break a demon's sigil?" I added.

Her brows pinched together as she looked from me to Ramona.

Very subtle, Iris!

"I thought only demons could break sigils." Citrine drummed her fingers across her lips. "And some other hell beasts. Vampires, maybe?"

"You're sure a witch wouldn't be powerful enough to conjure such a thing?" Ramona asked. Her hip grazed mine, reminding me how close to me she stood.

"Well, I didn't say that. With the right tools," Citrine said with a shrug. "And the right magical conduits."

"Like what?" Ramona growled, and I kicked her with my boot.

"I'm not sure. It depends on who they are and what access they have to the forces of nature or the supernatural," Citrine mused. "Sorry I can't be more helpful. Have you tried meditating and asking the goddess?"

"The goddess?" Ramona guffawed. "I'm still not talking to that—"

My elbow in Ramona's ribs stopped her from finishing that sentence. "That's okay," I amended. "It was worth a shot."

"You might try Dean at Midnight Market," Citrine suggested. "Have you met him yet? He's Billy Bacchus's nephew, new in town. Six foot seven, bright green. Buff. Hard to miss."

"Keep it in your pants, Citrine," Ramona muttered under her breath.

"Hmm?"

"Why should we go ask the new guy in town?" I interjected, once again saving Ramona from an underhanded comment.

Citrine shrugged. "Lots of demons in the town he moved here from. Apparently, he was a docent for the demonic council there. So maybe they had to deal with something like that in the past?"

"New in town. Interesting," Ramona said tightly, turning to leave before I could ask anything more.

"Oh, um, I should follow her." I hooked a thumb behind me and chased after Ramona.

"See you at the next coven meeting!" Citrine called after us.

Outside the shop, I caught up to Ramona quicker than I expected.

"Are you going to find this Dean guy?" I asked.

"I have no interest in tall green boys, no matter how buff," she snarked. "No, it's the demonic council I need to go talk to. I need to know if there's any new demons gracing Maple Hollow with a visit."

"Okay, well, where is the—"

"You can't come with me on this one, red."

"But we agreed I could help."

"The demonic council would eat you up, spit you out, and laugh at your masticated corpse."

I crossed my arms. "Well, that was a gross and entirely unnecessary description."

"Don't you have a day job? What about the apothecary?"

"Jordyn can handle the shop for a bit longer," I said with a wave. "Please?"

"Don't think that pouting will work on me." Ramona's eyes narrowed. "The only thing those pouty lips will get you is a trip to my playroom to meet my favorite flogger." I

nearly stumbled, choking on my own air, as Ramona continued, "And while I appreciate that your first instinct is to beg
for my attention, right now isn't a good time, witchling."

I reared back, heat filling my veins. "I . . . uh . . ."

Ramona laughed. "You look about ready to burst into
flames."

She started to walk away again.

For some reason, I desperately didn't want that to
happen, so I pulled out the last card I held: "But what about
our date?"

Ramona's slim frame whirled on me so fast I couldn't
react. She pinned me against the brick wall, her arms caging
me in so all I could see was the wicked smile on her red lips.

"Tempting me with your desperation?" she purred.

I trembled at the way her eyes snagged on my mouth. I
knew being with her would be so, *so* good, but a thrill of fear
ran along with my certainty. Most of the women in this
town I could handle with my eyes closed, but Ramona? I
might be out of my depth with Ramona.

"Name the place and time, witchling."

"Now," I rasped, wanting so badly to breach the distance
between our mouths. "I want to go with you to the demonic
council for our date." I had meant for it to be a "Gotcha!"
moment, but I was too flushed and turned on to pull it off.

"That's not a date, love, and you know it," she whispered, her breath hot on my lips as she leaned in. "A proper
date with me will end with you panting and begging for
more."

"You're making a lot of assumptions for someone who
had to coerce me into a date in the first place."

"You didn't take that much convincing. We both know
what you were secretly craving."

"A date doesn't have to end in sex," I added breathlessly even as I thought about all the ways she and I could intertwine, all the ways she could make me fall apart for her . . .

"No, but why deny the inevitable?" She leaned closer, and I resisted the urge to move before she pulled away. "Go have a long, cold shower, little witch. I've got work to do."

My body felt her absence before my other senses could catch up. She was halfway down the street before I could regain my footing. Lust and fire filled my veins. But instead of turning toward my apothecary and an ice-cold shower, I raced down another alleyway.

She wouldn't get away from me that easily.

10
RAMONA

The only person needing a fucking ice-cold shower was me. I'd never been so bothered without the satisfaction of torture or a climax.

Lucifer and the Seven Hells, those flushed cheeks, those pouty lips, those bedroom eyes.

I thought I knew a thing or two about torture, but that little witch was giving me a master class.

Iris was going to set me on fire. Frustration and impatience clouded my brain as I willed my legs to put more distance between her and me. I couldn't tell if I was more annoyed that she'd used our bargain as blackmail or that she'd done it poorly.

She thought she could trick me?

Me?

We would have to work on her manipulation skills if she was going to continue to be my little ginger shadow. I balled my hands into fists while I stormed through town, hoping I set the little witch on edge as much as she did me.

I made my way up the street, past the bakery. The

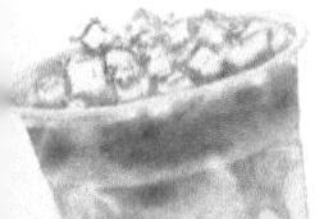

wolfman and his sister had a line out the door. Typical for the time of day, but now that there were two full-time bakers on the premises, it seemed to be the new hot spot in town. Content creators dressed in their stereotypical witchy garb held up their phones and cameras to record proof that they'd visited the spookily cute town of their dreams. Each of them angled their shots in an attempt to look like they hadn't been waiting in the cold for over an hour for the new wolf's specialties.

The quickest route was through the town square, so I crossed the street. Unfortunately, it was the peak time for tourists to frequent the coffee shop, bakery, and the other restaurants dotted about town.

"Ramona!" a shrill voice called from behind me. "Over here, yoo-hoo!"

I whipped my head around to find Lulu, the owner of the hair salon, running up the sidewalk while expertly evading the sightseers in her path. Her loud fuchsia hair was teased up into two buns today, and she wore matching eyeshadow and lipstick. Dressed in all dark green, she reminded me of a poisonous plant instead of a werewolf.

When she finally reached me, she doubled over and braced her hands on her thighs as she panted out the message that she'd deemed important enough to deliver in haste: "I got it. The hair gloss. The one I told you about. Last week."

"Okay?"

"I just got it in from Italy."

"I thought you were going to say the British are coming, for fuck's sake." I eyed her gripping the stitch in her side. "You could have just texted me. Are you trying out a new delivery service? Chasing down clients in the street?"

She straightened and giggled breathlessly. "I made a promise to let you know as soon as it came in. I know how particular you are about your products."

"Right. Well, I'll be in next week for my usual appointment." I took a step away, but she moved in front of me. "Is there something else I can help you with, Lulu?"

"Well, do you remember a few months back? You said if I ever wanted to discuss my . . . *future*"—she winked as if I didn't know what she was trying to say—"that you'd be receptive?"

What a day this was turning out to be.

Normally, I was the hunter. Today, the targets were chasing me down.

"Yes, Lulu." I resisted the urge to smile. I had been working on her for over a year and had almost given up. Now all I needed to do was reel her in. "You want to talk to me about that, beautiful?"

Her blush deepened. "I just—"

A loud, grating sound tore Lulu's attention away. Iris had appeared practically out of thin air, her arms crossed and a look of disgust on her face.

"Hey, Iris," Lulu said in greeting then turned back to me. "We can talk later. When you're free."

"I don't think that's a good idea, Lulu," Iris answered in my place. "Ramona is very busy at the moment and won't be free anytime soon. But how about you, Jordyn, and me have a girls' night? Nothing a night out at The Bloody Mary can't fix, right?"

What in the actual fuck was going on? Was she marking her territory? Or was she just trying to see how far she could push a demon into a crisis?

"Really?" Lulu beamed at the meddlesome witch. "That

would be wonderful, actually. You have no idea how lonely it can get at the salon."

"Come by the apothecary when you get off today," Iris said. "We'll make a plan."

Getting the clue that she'd been dismissed, Lulu smiled and bounced away . . . taking her as yet unclaimed soul with her.

"What was that about?" I snarled as soon as Lulu was out of earshot. "Are you trying to steal my catch?"

How the hell had Iris caught up to me so quickly? Were there magic portals in the alleys I didn't know about?

"Were you really going to let her sell her soul to you?" Iris whispered, irate. "In broad daylight? In front of *tourists*?"

"So, which part are you protesting, then?"

"What?"

"Are you mad that I was making a deal? That it was in broad daylight? *Or* are you mad that it was in front of tourists?"

"D. All of the above."

"Seven Hells," I muttered. "This is my literal job. 'Always be closing.' Did you think I only did deals in the dead of night, under a full moon?"

"Lulu is one of the sweetest people in town. And whatever the nymph needs, she can get on her own."

I wanted to clarify that Lulu was mostly werewolf and only *partially* nymph, but there was a more pressing matter at hand. "You interfered with my job, little witch. You better have a really good reason because I don't take kindly to people getting in the way of a fresh soul."

Her cheeks lit with a pink hue that spread to her neck. "We have a bigger job to do," Iris said, and I very much noted her liberal use of the word "we." "If you bartered for her soul, who's to say it wouldn't have been stolen out from under you like the others?"

My shoulders fell.

As much as I hated to admit it, she was right. Every soul waiting for collection would be in danger of being snatched away from me if I—*we*—didn't find out who was behind the thefts.

"Alright, then. Let's go, but you have to stay behind me. And don't say a single word. The last thing I need is you being mouthy and the demonic council deciding to take out their frustrations with you on me."

She made a gesture as if sealing her lips.

"Insufferable."

"You love it," she crooned, and my insides clenched.

"Yeah, I love little witches chasing my coattails and wanting to play detective. Delightful." I walked briskly in the direction of the council building. "Cost me another deal and you'll owe me more than just a date."

11

IRIS

I'd spent the better part of two days chasing after Ramona on this harebrained adventure, but even so, a little thrill filled me at the thought of actually seeing the demonic council. Getting a ticket to the inner sanctum was definitely above my pay grade as an apothecary witch. Had any witch ever stepped foot inside the place? Surely, I would've heard about it if someone had. I had been fully expecting Ramona to shut my request down when I'd scared off Lulu, but she'd crumbled relatively quickly for a stubborn demon.

Maybe I was finally working my charms on her? Witchful thinking. "Witchful Thinking" also happened to be the name of the local Maple Hollow therapist's office.

The way Ramona's eyes had flared bright with opportunity while she'd been talking to Lulu . . . I shuddered as I hastened to keep up with the long-legged temptress in front of me. Demons could feel the slightest sin bubbling under the surface. I couldn't help but wonder what sins Ramona sensed bubbling under mine.

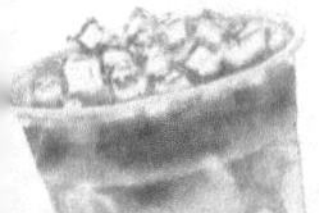

I cleared my throat. Better to not think of them in front of her.

We wove around the back of Bones and Tomes Bookstore, stacks of empty boxes piled up on either side of the forest-green door, waiting to be recycled. Across the narrow road was a nondescript burgundy door, Latin written on gold plating across it. I'd walked past that door a million times, had even opened it once to see what was inside, only to find a cloakroom, but I hadn't dared to step over the threshold, lest I be sucked straight to hell. I imagined there was a false door that was opened by some demonic incantation, but I wasn't about to get on the demons' wrong side by trying to find a way in uninvited.

Now, I was getting a personal escort.

Ramona and I walked into a dark chamber, lit only by a large brass lantern hanging from the ceiling.

"I'd offer to take your jacket," Ramona said, "but I'm assuming your macrame waistcoat is at the cleaners?"

I rolled my eyes but didn't miss the way the buttons on her white shirt strained across her chest as she shrugged off her woolen trench. The loose silk fabric slouched back into place as she hung her garment up, and I realized that I'd never been so attentive to the quality of clothing on anyone else. There was no shortage of rich men who paraded their stylish families around town during their visits, but none of them made luxury look so *appealing*.

"It's not even that cold," I rebuffed, even as I shuddered at a sudden chill that swept through the crack in the door. "I won't be whipping out the heavy coats until past All Hallow's." I crooked a brow at Ramona as she hung her coat amongst a line of near-identical ones. "I suppose demons are used to hotter weather."

She let out a surprised laugh and looked back at me with a wink. "Something like that."

"Goddess, we're not about to enter *hell*-hell, are we?"

"*Hell*-hell? As opposed to Hell Lite? Diet Hell?"

My eyes darted to her. "Are we going to actual, literal Hell right now?"

She grinned. "Would that frighten you?"

"No"—I groaned—"but I would've worn a nicer outfit." I pulled at my turtleneck. "I knew I should've worn the emerald skirt. It really brings out my eyes and—" Ramona looked at me, perplexed. "What?"

"Nothing. You just say the oddest things at times." She straightened the cuffs on her shirt and rolled her shoulders back. "Remember, stay behind me. Don't talk."

"Stay behind you. Don't talk. Got it." I gave her an awkward thumbs-up that made Ramona look even more exasperated.

She faced the back wall. Holding up her hand, she said, "*Ego sum ex hoc velo.*"

With a groaning pop, the wall sank in and rolled to the side, revealing a giant hallway. I gasped, taking in the opulent space.

This was nothing like the dark, little speakeasy I'd expected. No, this place was a towering hall of white and black marble flecked with silver and gold, black sconces, and black and burgundy velvet upholstery. If Mount Olympus and Transylvania had a demonic palace baby, this is what it would look like.

It was notably warmer in here than it was outside, and I wondered if they intentionally kept it balmy so it felt more like *home.*

"Let's go, red," Ramona said, tipping her head toward

the giant stairwell at the far end of the hall. Giant fireplaces roared to life on either side of the hall when she stepped onto the marble floor, her dress shoes clicking, one step, two, before she paused and turned toward me with a smirk.

"Wow," was all I could manage as I followed her. My body felt light, nearly floating in the cavernous space.

How was this here, hidden down a tiny street in a sleepy little town?

Footsteps echoed from up ahead, and I craned my neck up to see Naphula standing on the balcony, scowling down at us. I only knew her in passing, had heard more whispers about her than words she'd actually spoken from her own mouth. Witches and demons weren't exactly meant to consort—not that I held that reminder in any regard, obviously—but Naphula didn't fraternize with *any* witches in town as far as I knew.

"What is *she* doing here?" the silver-haired demon asked venomously.

"Ignore my new pet," Ramona announced to her friend. "I came to speak with the council."

"I'm not your pet," I hissed at her under my breath.

Ramona spun to glare at me, and the rest of the words I'd been about to say disappeared from my lips. I'd given her a promise that I wouldn't speak—*twice*—and had broken it within moments. She looked away before the scarlet shame radiating from my belly could reach my cheeks. I was beginning to recognize that I had put myself in real danger by being here. This council chamber was beyond the coven's purview. There would be no rescue if things went awry, and I wasn't sure that Ramona could help much either.

Naphula tsked, shaking her head disapprovingly. "Are you fucking this one too?"

I bristled at that but bit my tongue to remain silent. Was this something Ramona did often? Broker deals and then lure her marks into her bed? Woo them with trips to the demonic council? Would she have slept with Lulu if I hadn't intervened?

It shouldn't have bothered me in the slightest. It was probably the least objectionable thing about the demon, especially considering my own body count. Still, for a moment I had felt like I was special, and now I felt like just another fool pulled in by her overpowering charisma.

Instead of answering Naphula's accusatory question, Ramona only repeated, "I am here to request a favor of the council. I only need a few moments of their time."

Naphula rounded a banister and started slowly walking down the obsidian stairs to meet us. Each step was etched with gold scenes that were hard to make out but made me uneasy, nonetheless. When her sharp heels hit the main floor, she paused several feet away and looked me over. I could feel the judgment radiating from her. Whether she was displeased that her friend brought me into their sacred space or that I existed at all was up for question.

"They are fully booked today," Naphula said, crossing her arms over her chest. "You will need to reschedule. Perhaps I can be of help?"

Ramona let out a frustrated sound, her shoulders drooping. "You already know why I'm here." She sounded pained to admit it. "My missing souls."

"Souls?" Naphula asked, eyes darting from Ramona to me and back. "As in plural?"

"The old innkeeper's soul has been pilfered as well," Ramona admitted.

"Shit," Naphula replied tightly. "Why didn't you call me?"

"You never answer your fucking phone anymore." The muscle in Ramona's jaw worked. "Besides, I thought I had it handled." Her eyes shifted down to me. "There's got to be some way to track these souls down. They didn't just vanish into the ether. Someone took them. And if they're not in hell, they're being held somewhere else."

"Tracking souls . . ." Naphula shook her head. "That's well above our clearance."

"Yes," Ramona gritted out. "Which is why we're here."

A look of exasperation crossed Naphula's cold face. "If you want to interrupt their meeting, I'm sure their displeasure will make quite the show."

"It would be for a good reason," Ramona countered.

Naphula inspected her fingernails, feigning boredom to make her point—something Ramona did often as well. "Indeed. And Dominic will be very excited to inspect a soul marked with your sigil." Her midnight eyes slid to me. "Especially since such souls are being snatched right out from under your nose."

Ramona's lip curled in disgust. "I think it's best that I come back at a later time. *Without* the witch."

"Good thinking." Naphula smiled at Ramona, proud of herself for her victory over Ramona's ego. "But I'll let them know that *you* stopped by."

I knew, in her own way, that Naphula was trying to protect Ramona—and me by extension.

Ramona hooked her hand around my elbow and steered me away. "Let's go."

As I followed her to the magical exit, I thought back to the comment Ramona had made about tracking the missing souls. After all, there were stacks of spell books at the apothecary full of locator spells. My mind started whirling. It would take time, but there had to be something in those books we could use to summon one of the missing souls. Witches used soul summoning all the time. Jordyn's mishap last year wasn't typical, but I would heed that experience.

Maybe I could find a spell that could tell us who had stolen Ramona's souls?

We didn't need another Lou situation on our hands, but summoning Saul or Maude for a short time couldn't hurt. If I could find a way to tweak the spell so that I could pull a bound soul to me, maybe they could tell me who'd come for them. Even if they didn't remember, maybe there'd be a magical fingerprint left on them by the culprit.

"I have a plan," I announced once the crisp air of the outside world pushed into my lungs.

Ramona looked over her shoulder at the door she'd just sealed. Only the thin outline of the secret opening remained.

"Whatever you're going to say, don't," she said before I could even get a word out. "I have no more time to discuss your foolish schemes or whacky, witchy what-have-yous."

"What?" I looked around the silent street as if I'd find an answer written across the red brick. "You don't want to hear my plan?"

What had changed in the matter of minutes we'd spent in the demonic council chambers?

Something like fear flashed behind Ramona's eyes. She seemed rattled, but by what, I didn't know. When Naphula had mentioned Dominic and the fact that I also bore her sigil . . .

She placed her hand on my lower back and guided me to the middle of the town square before she spoke. The witch-hat gazebo was inundated with tourists using it as a backdrop for their family photos. Ramona stopped in front of me, blocking us from prospective photo bombs.

Why did she need me to be out in the open for whatever she was about to say? This felt like some douchebag breakup strategy.

Then she looked at me, her brows knitted in concern, and my stomach clenched.

"This is dangerous, Iris," she said. "More dangerous than you know. I never should've roped you into this. The best thing you can do to help is to stay away until I figure out who has been snatching these souls."

Seeing Ramona sweat should have made me realize the severity of the situation, but it only made me want to fight harder. We were getting close to answers—I could feel it. What's more, I was angry. When was Ramona going to stop treating me like a damsel in distress and like the powerful witch I was?

"Ooh, so chivalrous," I snarked, waving jazz hands. "I may like apple picking and wearing cute sweaters, demon, but I can handle danger."

"Not this kind." Ramona shook her head. "I don't want you on the other demons' radars. We still don't have any leads, and the more we question people, the more likely the person behind this will figure out that we're looking for them. We'll lose the upper hand—"

"But I have an idea—" I started.

"Everyone in town is a suspect. And if they decide to come after all of my souls, that means they'll come after you—"

"Ramona, just listen. I could summon the soul of Saul or Maude and ask them what happened—"

"No!" she barked. "If they are still bound to the person who snatched them, then they will know it was you who cast the spell. They can't know you're involved in this. Just stay in the apothecary where you are warded and safe."

"Why do you care if they know it was me?" I balked. "Who cares if it puts me in danger?"

"I care!" she shouted, and I froze at the force of her words. "I care, dammit. Iris, please just leave this alone."

With that, she stormed back toward the demonic council, leaving me reeling. A small crowd of strangers looked at me as if I'd just been dumped.

And in a way, they were right.

12

RAMONA

I never should've put her in that kind of danger. *What was I thinking?* As I retraced my steps, my fury rose until I was drowning in all the things I shouldn't have done. Including waiting for Iris to storm off toward the apothecary so I could reenter the demonic council without her.

I straightened my coat, trying not to think of that look in her eyes. A good demon would've taken her help, put her in harm's way, let her get herself killed. I shouldn't care. But apparently, there were some things that I refused to waste, use, and abuse. Most souls, I wanted to hunt, but Iris's, I wanted to protect. And I wasn't willing to examine that thought any further.

Charging back through the hall and into the atrium, I spotted Naphula leaning against the pillar at the foot of the stairs. "I had a feeling you'd need backup," she said and held out her hand.

Naphula made a fist then opened it again a moment later. In a flash of magic, a large pastry box appeared in the

air before it delicately landed in her outstretched palm. "Apple cider donut?"

I gave her a quizzical look.

She'd never been one for sweets, but my old friend clearly knew my penchant for them. I appreciated the thought after several shitty days in a row. And I suspected it wasn't a great hardship for her to visit the beautiful were-wolf baker who seemed to have snagged her attention.

"Where did you manage to get those?" I asked.

She grinned. "The bakery, of course."

"No, those." I pointed to the marks on her forearm that peeked out from her sleeve. The flesh looked like it was freshly healed with a bright pink hue.

"It's nothing." She pulled her arm back, but I wasn't going to let her get away without explaining.

"Aw, come on, Naphula, tell me. You getting freaky with that succubus again?"

She pursed her lips, her brow pinched, and challenged my power of will. "A one-night tryst *may* have gotten out of hand."

I winked at her. "I knew it."

With a laugh, she opened the box and handed me a still-warm donut. The wafting scent of cinnamon and melted butter made me salivate. "Before you cross the void and get the both of us in trouble for not being able to handle our shit here on this plane, run through your plan with me, okay?"

I bit into the soft crumb and savored it, disregarding the granules of sugar that fell onto my lapels. "There are a few bounty hunters in hell who could help us," I mused.

"What outcome are you hoping for, Mona? Because I have a feeling Billy will not be happy if a horde of demon underlings swarms the town looking for a needle in all his decorative fucking haystacks."

"I still have solutions. This isn't a lost battle, even though I still appreciate the consolation pastries. Who's the top hunter these days?" I knew that the threat of souls being taken out from under me was a more serious matter than employing a freelancer. "Shax, perhaps?"

Naphula smirked. "And if he hunted down the culprit to that little witch's door?"

My mouth went dry midchew. "It wasn't her."

"She cozied up to you rather quickly after that first soul was snatched," she countered.

"She's just bored," I said flippantly.

"Are you sure she wasn't trying to get your attention? You can't trust the witches, Mona. You know this."

"She doesn't want information. And there's no way she was the soul thief. She just wants something to do."

I already knew what Naphula would say.

"The full swing of seasonal tourism isn't enough to keep her busy?" she asked. "Or the thousand other beings who live here who are far more interesting than you? No offense."

"None taken."

"She wants to chase after the local demon with no ulterior motive? I mean, don't get me wrong, Mona, you're hot shit, but there are a hundred other paranormals that Iris could be chasing after if she just wanted a woman who was hot and magical, you know?"

Silence fell over us. I had no answer to that. Iris could have started a new hobby or thrown herself into a committee. Lucifer knows that Billy Bacchus and the other town elders were always harping about civic duty and getting more involved with town events. I knew boredom wasn't the only reason. But a quiet, ashamed part of me had hoped there was another reason why Iris wanted my attention, something beyond one salacious night. I hated that I'd even had the thought.

I clenched my jaw and set those wishy-washy notions aside.

"Fine, let's not beat around the bush any longer." Naphula's sharp tone cut through the room, pulling my attention back. "I think you should cut all ties with the witch until you figure out who exactly is threatening your job. Fuck her after—"

I let out a growl. "Don't talk about her like that."

"Oh, Mona." Naphula let out a mocking laugh. "You can't afford to be distracted by worthless feelings and passing crushes."

"I don't have crushes."

"You're right. You either fuck them once or you love them so deeply that the world practically implodes when it ends. The last woman you pursued was so intense that when it was over, you were pure bloody chaos to deal with for three whole decades."

That memory stung.

"Please listen to me," Naphula implored. "L—" I gave her a sharp look, and she recalculated using the *L* word. "Romance, especially right now, is a distraction you can't afford. You have too much at stake."

I didn't need the reminder.

"Then where should I go, if not to the council?" I sighed in frustration. "I have nothing to go on. No trail to track."

"You're friendly with the local vampire group, right? Those bloodsuckers are always in everyone's business."

I groaned. I hadn't wanted to pull the vampires—or

anyone else for that matter—into this, but Naphula was right. Agnes knew everything about everyone. She could tell you their favorite drink, their latest kink, and how regular their bowel movements were. And I knew exactly where she'd be tomorrow.

"Thanks for the pep talk." I tapped the box. "And the donuts." Turning on my heel, I threw over my shoulder to my friend, "And if you're going to sleep with werewolves, you should really invest in chainmail first."

She grumbled a low, "Noted."

13
IRIS

"Lavender matcha latte?" Harlow offered, sliding the drink across the corner booth.

It had been three days since the demonic council. In my perpetual stubbornness, I'd decided that my only course of action was to continue the soul-snatching investigation from afar. And the best way I knew how to do that was through stacks and stacks of old books.

Harlow dropped into the seat opposite me and eyed the mountain of dusty tomes strewn about the table along with notebooks filled with my frantic chicken-scratch writing.

"If you need me to move, just say so," I said wearily, my eyes stinging from staring at the faded cursive for hours.

"We don't need you to move," Harlow replied. "Not that many people are looking for cinnamon crumble muffins and flat whites at"—she looked at her watch—"eight o'clock at night. Stay as long as you like, but we are closing soon, just so you know."

"What?" I exclaimed, looking up at the clock mounted

above the register and then to the upturned chairs and freshly mopped floors. "Goddess." I rubbed my eyes, suddenly realizing I'd been deep in focus for hours. "You closed up ages ago."

Harlow waved a hand. "It's fine. You seemed like you were in a trance or something, and I didn't want to interrupt." She slid a plate of pastries across the table—one I hadn't even realized was there. "Muffin?"

"Thanks." I only realized that I was hungry when the smell of apple butter and walnut crumble filled my senses. "I appreciate it," I added through a mouthful.

"Everything okay?" Harlow hedged.

"Yep."

This wasn't the first time I'd used research as a coping mechanism. A good deep dive into the pages of books older than my grandmother always healed my worrying mind.

Well, it usually did.

Tonight, I was left with more questions than answers.

I was still grappling with what Ramona had said, that she "cared" about me but didn't want me around anymore. What was I supposed to do with that? What did it even mean? I didn't know, but goddess, it meant *something*, and my anxious brain was determined to distract me from examining it any further by doing an entire PhD amount of research in three days.

The echoes of that moment rattled through me, filling me with equal parts excitement and dread. Whenever I was around her, I was free-falling, just waiting for when I would finally land, and when I did, when she and I collided, I knew it would be earth-shaking.

When Harlow didn't move, I peeked up from my studies,

chipmunk cheeks full. "Is there something else you wanted?"

"Oh no." She didn't move. "It's just . . . well . . . I just wanted to make sure you weren't mad at me?" She pressed her lips together as if trying to keep the word vomit at bay, but she couldn't help herself and it all tumbled out. "I mean, this might just be an ADHD thing, or maybe I'm really missing the whole picture, but it seems like you are really unhappy every time I come around lately, and we used to be tight, but now it seems less so, and I know it's probably my fault. Jordyn and I have been having a lot of solo time, but I never wanted to make you feel left out. It's just between shifts at the café and the apothecary, we get so little time together, and I want you to have your friend time and I want us to have our friend time too, 'cause we're still friends, or at least I hope we are—"

I reached out and grabbed her wrist. "Breathe," I instructed with all of my apothecary healer calm.

She took a deep, gulping breath, face red as she panted. "Sorry."

"You are my friend," I said slowly so her overwhelmed mind could hear me. "And I have been a little surlier than usual about your relationship, if I'm being honest. But it's not your fault at all. It's a me thing. I just feel kind of lonely and left out, I guess."

Harlow nodded. "You're important to me, to us, Iris. We should make more time to be together. Or at least, I'd like that."

"I'd like that too," I admitted.

Willow stormed through the back door, jolting us out of the conversation. She slammed the door behind her and locked it.

"Jeez, Willow, you okay?" Harlow asked.

"Don't follow me!" Willow screeched, her voice sounding watery, as if she'd been crying. Harlow stood, and Willow, even though she'd disappeared upstairs to her apartment, called, "Seriously, Harlow. I want to be left alone right now."

Harlow slumped back down, her brows pinched in concern.

"Where was she coming from?" I asked.

"She said she was going to drop something off at the bakery," Harlow replied. "I don't know. You think . . ." She eyed me. "Something happened between her and Wyatt? I mean, I know they're not officially together, but maybe she caught him with someone else?"

"We're talking about the baker, right?" My eyes flared in confusion. "Wyatt? The werewolf with puppy-dog eyes who looks at your sister like she hung the moon? That Wyatt?"

"Yeah, you're right," Harlow muttered. "That can't be it."

"Are they even together? Like, I keep thinking they are, but—"

"Willow hasn't told me anything," Harlow admitted, seemingly hurt that her sister would keep such things a secret. But maybe they didn't even see it themselves yet. Sometimes a person could have a freaking "I love you" sign stapled to their forehead and the other person still wouldn't believe it. "But I did catch them hugging through the window of the bakery the other night," Harlow added. "So, I know that something is going on there, but as of yet, not a single Maple Hollow resident has seen them kiss, so . . ."

"If they did, someone in town would know." I snorted. "I'm surprised there's not more gossip. Everyone in this town knows everyone else's business." I took another bite of my muffin. "Oh, by the way, Randy has formally requested that you and Jordyn stop hooking up in the pumpkin patch."

Harlow made a choking sound right as the front door's lock magically flipped and Jordyn walked in.

"Hey, it's my two favorite people!" she called. She wandered over, slid into the booth beside Harlow, then planted a kiss on her girlfriend's lips. "You ready for our date?"

I did my very best to keep my smile warm and neutral, even as my mood soured.

"Change of plans," Harlow said, kissing Jordyn on the temple. "We're going to be helping Iris tonight with"—she waved her hand over my stack of books—"whatever this is."

"Sweet," Jordyn said. "I haven't had a good Iris info dump in ages. What are we researching?"

I blinked. *Simple as that?* I suddenly realized how easy it would've been to ask them to hang out, to invite them to spend more time with me. I'd been just as guilty of pulling away as they were. It was a much-needed course correction in my brain: My friends *wanted* to spend time with me. All I needed to do was ask.

"So what exactly is this?" Jordyn asked, picking up a tome of summoning rituals. "Oh goddess, you're not thinking of summoning a hexed spirit, are you?"

"It turned out so well last time," Harlow snarked.

"Hey, I am not the one with a history of botched summonings," I said pointedly, and Jordyn laughed. "Besides, this is different."

"Oh boy, this should be interesting." Jordyn started stacking up the books. "Okay, no summoning spells in the café. Let's head back to the Poison Apple." She gave me a look. "I want you to know that I do not condone this."

"But you're going to help me anyway, aren't you?" I taunted.

She let out a long-suffering sigh. "Yep, let's go. Harlow, grab the leftover pastries from the cake case. It's going to be a long night."

14
RAMONA

Normally, the smell of death in the air brought me nothing but joy, but when I felt Lyra's soul separate from her body, it brought me nothing but dread. Three deals coming to fruition in one week wasn't just unusual, it was too suspicious to be a coincidence. Everything I once felt with assurance now wavered. Would my sigil still be on her skin? Would I be faced with yet another failure?

Over a week had passed since the first soul has been taken from me. Trying to find the soul thief was leading me to fruitless dead ends and in infuriating circles. The last three days in particular had been insufferably long . . . and I was determined *not* to think about if the absence of a certain witch had made them feel even longer.

I was halfway across the graveyard when a flashlight beam hit me straight in the eyes. I lifted a hand with a snarl as an echoing voice called, "Stop knocking boots in my graveyard, Dean. People live here, you know."

"I'm not knocking anyone's boots here, Randy," I called

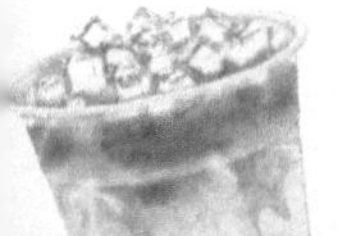

back. "The last thing I need is some supernatural STI. I've got business to attend to."

"Ah, Ramona," the monster called back.

He lowered his flashlight, revealing he was perched on a stool opposite his cousin, Rudy, a half-finished game of cards between them. An old wooden sign propped up on an apple barrel served as their makeshift table. Several empty beer bottles were scattered around the tall grass. The mausoleum that Randy had moved into was wide open behind them. With my eyes adjusting to the light, I could make out his plush cot where the previous resident's coffin had sat.

Nothing like two pumpkin monsters having a card game in the middle of a graveyard . . .

Yep, of all the towns I'd ever lived in, Maple Hollow was officially the strangest.

"Evening, Rudy," I called to the town medical examiner. He was one of the chattiest busybodies around. He even gave Agnes a run for her money.

Rudy saluted two long fingers off the brow of his orange head. "How's it shaking, troublemaker? Hell keeping you busy?"

I rolled my eyes. Rudy was the epitome of dad energy.

"It's a nice night for a walk," I replied, straightening my spine and slipping my hands into my pockets. "I have business with the recently departed Lyra."

"Lyra died?" Randy's voice pitched in his surprise. "And here I was certain she would make it to nine hundred."

"Folks are dropping like fireflies these days," Rudy interjected. "Hope we don't have another you-know-what on our hands. That was a lot of messy paperwork trying to fudge those details."

"Hell forbid you have to do your job," I mumbled to myself. What was the earshot like on pumpkin heads, anyway?

"You had a deal with ol' Lyra then, eh, Ramona?" Randy stood and dusted his hands on his jeans. "She was quite the looker."

"Such was her nature," I replied tightly. "Have a good evening, gentlemen."

"If you come across any wayward teens on your way through the graves, tell 'em to scram, will ya? I hate to be a downer, but the ghouls and lingering spirits get all riled up and keep me awake all night."

I huffed a laugh at that. "I'll demand you get your beauty sleep."

"Amen," Rudy mocked with a whistle. "You're looking terrible these days, cousin. Losing your deep orange hue."

"If the lack of sleep involved me getting laid, I wouldn't be such a sour squash," Randy added with a snicker. "But I haven't been able to get to second base without having to chase off some horny townies. Sort of dampens the mood, if you know what I mean."

"Gross," I grumbled as I wandered toward the mausoleum without a formal goodbye. "I feel like I need to take a shower."

I wandered under a twisted, old elm, its dead leaves brushing my shoulders as I crested the hill of the graveyard and down the other side, to where the larger family plots resided. Lyra had taken up residence here about a century ago and had sold her soul to me for a constant supply of food. I'd made Lyra promise to eat only the out-of-towners, but a reclusive succubus could only do so much.

The ivy and moss-covered stone of her former home

turned eternal resting place came into view, the door left ajar. I pushed it open, and the smell of earth, rot, and death met me in an instant. Her remains lay in the stone sarcophagus in the middle of the space, beautiful and terrifying no more. Her vacant white eyes stared up at the marbled ceiling, and her greyscaly skin was stretched tight over her bones that would likely turn to ash in a matter of days.

"So long, old friend." I spoke softly, not wanting to wake any other dead.

Succubi were creatures of hell, after all. Created to feast on the lust of the unchaste. The bones of those whose life forces she'd drained were littered about the swamp. As far as monsters went, she'd been a clean-and-kept one who'd never shat where she ate. Something more of us should have learned by now.

After bidding her vessel a final farewell, I looked around for what I'd come for: the sigil on her bare thigh.

It was still *unbroken.*

A warm glow peeked out from behind the stone container and lifted into the air before me as if drawn to my power. The golden orb vibrated until I reached out my palm, giving it a place to land.

Lyra's soul.

Thank every fucking devil in hell.

A huge wave of relief hit me when I pocketed the orb. Whoever had stolen the other two souls was still out there, but they weren't as close on my tail as I'd feared. I could handle someone in my orbit as long as they didn't have all of my most intimate deals on their radar. Saul and Maude had been humans. Maybe this thief couldn't track my paranormal clients as easily?

Green eyes and brilliant red hair shouldn't have flashed

through my mind, nor the feeling of melancholy. I'd sent the witch away, and it had been the right thing to do. No more Watson to my Sherlock. She should be safe as long as only a few people had seen us together. Safe with her coven, safe with her warnings, safe if we could manage to keep our distance.

But can I actually do that?

I judged my own resistance to the draw she had on me. Maybe I was spelled? An obsession spell that she'd placed on me the second time we'd kissed? That had to be it. I prided myself on my immaculate self-control. No one riled me up these days. I'd put all that burning passion to bed long ago.

Seven Hells, what I would give to kiss her again.

Fuck!

The little witch had completely warped my mind.

No.

I was determined to figure out who was behind these soul snatchings and get back to being the terrifying demon I'd always been. I might even take Agnes up on her offer to meet her at the club again and return my life to its normal equilibrium.

No more witches.

After calling in the deal I'd made with Iris, we would go back to being strangers who happened to live in the same enchanted town. Nothing more. That was exactly what I would do.

With renewed confidence and my brokered soul in hand, I wandered through the graveyard, determined not to think about the green-eyed witch and all the chaos she left in her wake.

15
IRIS

We fell into a well-worn rhythm as Jordyn and Harlow helped me gather all the supplies for the summoning. They'd clearly seen my mountain of dusty tomes in the diner as a cry for help, and we went straight back to the apartment to get to work. I hadn't realized how much I'd missed this until we were doing it again—performing spells, working through the night, hunting clues.

It had taken us hours to find something that Maude Ketchum had been attached to in life. The B&B was full of knickknacks, antiques, and random heirlooms, but we needed something that had truly been hers, something that she'd cherished, which had made the task almost impossible.

Understandably, Jordyn was extra careful with our prep this time. No wine was permitted pre-ritual. The last thing we needed was another sloppy summoning. Jordyn's experience last year with Lou had shaken her confidence with this

type of magic. Harlow, on the other hand, was like an excited golden retriever. She had the good sense not to pepper her girlfriend with a million questions about magic but seemed to have no issue asking me.

"Why salt?" Harlow asked, stir-fried noodles hanging from her overloaded mouth.

Summoning on an empty stomach was not good practice, and we had a few hours before midnight, so we'd ordered dinner from the local noodle shop. After that, we'd spent probably way too long double-checking the incantations and candle placements.

"It's a purification thing," Jordyn answered. "Even the best intentions can be muddied if the spell area isn't purified properly." She pointed her chopsticks at me. "It also helps if you have more than one witch present to keep the vibes on task. It's easy to let emotions and the spirit get a bit . . . out of hand."

I wanted to point out that Lou, her ex-girlfriend, being stuck on our plane for so long had had more to do with Lou's unsolved murder than Jordyn's emotions getting out of hand, but I knew Jordyn still bore the burden of responsibility. And Lou was at peace now because of Jordyn—something she might've never gotten if Jordyn hadn't been a witch.

Harlow scooped another bundle of noodles into her mouth, nodding at her paramour.

"We shouldn't need to hold onto Maude for long," Jordyn said. "Just one question."

"What do you need to ask her?" Harlow asked.

I took a deep breath. They needed to know before the ritual started. This would help us properly set the intentions, but would also keep the encounter on track once Maude crossed the veil.

Bracing myself for their reactions, I started spilling my guts. "Ramona's souls are being stolen. The person responsible has figured out a way of breaking Ramona's sigil and snatching the souls before Ramona can collect them."

I waited for the other shoe to drop while they sat there blinking at me.

And waited . . .

And waited . . .

When neither said anything, I continued, "The last soul that was stolen was Maude Ketchum's, so I want to call hers forth her and hopefully she can tell us who broke the sigil before she passed away. So only one question: who?"

"Okay." Jordyn looked between Harlow and me. "So explain to me *why* we're helping Ramona again? Meddling in demon affairs is dangerous, Iris. You know the coven wouldn't approve. Hell, I don't approve! Are you sure you want to get further wrapped up in her world?"

I shrugged, feigning casual interest. "She's part of our town."

"You're suddenly concerned with being an upstanding citizen?"

"Yeah," Harlow chimed in. "I mean, Ramona also tricked you into making a deal with her. Is this part of that? Do you owe her this? If so, this is a pretty lousy date."

"It's sort of part of it," I hedged. "She didn't actually ask for my help, but Ramona is . . . guarded. This whole thing has her really riled. She seemed upset, and she wouldn't let a witch help if she didn't really need it. Right?"

"Oh, so this is because you like her," Jordyn cut in. "I thought you swore to me no demons?"

"No—I mean, yes, but no." I stumbled over my words with absolutely no grace. "This isn't about liking her. If I even did, which I don't. Definitely not. Not really."

"Oh, you're down bad!" Harlow jeered.

Shit. This was the last thing I needed.

I shook my head and held up my hands. "Okay, don't be mad, but it's a little more complicated, and I didn't want to tell you guys, but . . ." I pulled back the collar of my shirt and showed them the mark on my clavicle. "I'm a little more involved than just helping her out."

Jordyn lunged closer and rubbed two fingers over the mark as if trying to check that it was permanent. "This is much bigger than you let on. I didn't think she marked you with that deal for information last year."

"She didn't."

"Then why do you have a demon sigil on your skin?" Jordyn screeched.

"It happened when we extended the deal over the summer."

"What!" Jordyn shouted. "You made *another* deal with her? Damn it, Iris!"

Ichabod leaped off the couch, and Harlow slung an arm around Jordyn's shoulder to calm her down.

Jordyn took a breath and in a calmer voice asked, "Why didn't you tell us about the mark sooner?"

I pulled out of her reach and fixed my clothes to cover up the mark again. "Because it was already done and it'll be removed once the deal is completed—I checked a dozen times—so I didn't think it would matter. So, I have her mark on me for a bit. It'll be gone soon. It's not forever! Think of it like a really long-lasting temporary tattoo."

Jordyn pinched the bridge of her nose. "Okay, so there's

much more of a vested interest in this soul stealing than we originally thought.”

“Yeah, we have to figure out who this thief is. They could come after you next,” Harlow said, her voice deeper and more serious now.

“They’re only going after souls that are passing naturally,” I assured them. “Otherwise, it would be too hard to hide. Everyone would be on high alert if someone were going around and killing anyone in association with Ramona.” My words didn’t seem to comfort them. “And besides, if we figure out who it is tonight, then they’ll be stopped long before they can get to me.”

Jordyn crossed her arms, clearly unhappy but cognizant of the rock and hard place I was stuck between. “Fine, but she owes you big time after this. That date better be the best date ever in the existence of dates, and after, she is never to speak to you again.”

“Really good dates between women never end with never speaking again, babe.” Harlow laughed. “They end with the strap—”

“Don’t you dare finish that thought,” Jordyn warned with a pointed finger.

I rolled my eyes as if I didn’t already know.

The mood warmed from there. I was relieved to ease back into a less stressful conversation than Jordyn looking at me like I was a coven traitor. They told me about some local gossip they’d heard and their plans for a trip to one of the magical Christmas towns up north for the holidays. It was as if no time had passed between us, even though I couldn’t remember the last time we’d hung out like this. Eventually, Ichabod curled up on my lap, well aware of what time we usually headed to bed.

Rhythmically petting the soft fur on the top of his head soothed him long enough for the old grandfather clock in the corner to strike midnight.

It was finally time.

Jordyn and Harlow pushed the couch out of the way, then rolled up the large rug to avoid any stray candle wax dripping onto it—and to spare us twenty minutes of vacuuming salt out of its soft fibers.

Jordyn and I chanted a protection spell as we drew the salt circle, marked the compass points with chalk and protective herbs, and laid out our offerings. Maude's favorite sugar bowl sat in the middle, along with a small tray of sweets from Midnight Market and a bundle of herbs to burn after she moved on again.

Maude's daughter thought that we were borrowing the dish to pay her spirit homage and bless her journey across the veil. *Which* technically wasn't a lie since Jordyn had promised we would do it after we got our answers. Maude would haunt us for sure if we damaged it, and the apothecary really didn't need that kind of poltergeist energy hanging around . . . again.

Jordyn and Harlow joined me in the circle, and we joined hands. I began the chant, followed by Jordyn. Harlow, still learning Latin and spell binding, only hummed and focused all her intentions on Maude joining the circle with us.

"*Coniuro te. Veni ad regnum nostrum, et loquere veritatem tuam,*" Jordyn and I chanted in unison until the candles around the circle started to flicker.

The room went still.

Goose bumps erupted up my arms and the back of my neck. A blurred image of mousy brown hair, wrinkled skin, and a fluffy cheetah-print robe came into focus.

"Maude, we've summoned your spirit tonight to ask for your help," I said. "Would you be willing?"

It was a formal-sounding request, but I promised Jordyn we'd play this by the book.

"That doesn't look like Maude," I heard Harlow whisper to Jordyn, who shushed her quickly. But it was too late.

Maude's wispy form rounded on Harlow and gave her the stink eye. "If you must know, my body didn't age, but my soul was well worn." Maude dabbed at the bags under her eyes as if vanity had gotten the better of her, even in death. "That demon's magic only worked until I was detached from my mortal vessel."

"I'm so sorry. I didn't—"

"Please, Maude," I cut in, trying to reel the situation back in. "When your soul left your body, were you alone? Or did someone visit before you passed?"

The transparent figure floated higher and leisurely twisted around before hanging upside down in front of my face. Her long, withered finger pointed at me.

"I saw you there. After," she said, her voice creaky. "With Ramona."

"Yes, but before that? Did anyone else come to see you?"

She slowly rotated as if on an axis, her lips pursed. "There was someone. With long teeth. I remember the table lamplight glinting off them as she laughed. Sweet girl, but a little too chatty for my liking." Her image flickered in and out of focus.

"Who? Who was the chatty woman?" I perked up, squeezing Jordyn and Harlow's hands tighter so Maude wouldn't slip away.

"She had big hair, wavy brown. Blue eyes and a fiery personality. But I didn't recognize her."

"Is there anything else about her that you can tell us?" Jordyn asked. "Did she say a name or where she lives?"

Maude floated closer to the ceiling. "I don't know any of that. But she talked like Ramona. Cocky. And a bit uppity. The immortals always are."

"Immortal with long teeth?" Harlow whispered toward me. "Does she mean the vampires? Could it be a vamp?"

"Maybe?"

We all watched Maude continue to turn about as she started singing a haunting tune to herself.

Ichabod jumped onto the couch and mewed at Maude, who wiggled a loose thread from her shawl. He happily batted at it.

"Wouldn't she know if it was one of the local vampires? She and Agnes manned the welcome booth together for years," Jordyn reminded me. "Ask her where she is. Who holds the strings to her soul now that she's been cut loose from Ramona?"

"Could you—" I made to ask another question when the cat leaped through Maude's body, landed on the edge of the circle, and went sliding across the floor through the line of salt.

In an instant, Maude's ghost was gone and the candles all went out, casting us into darkness.

Harlow bolted to the nearest lamp. "Is she gone? Should we try to call her back?" Her eyes searched the room, but Jordyn was already lighting the cleansing herbs.

"It's better that we don't," Jordyn said, trailing smoke around the living room. "Calling her back that quickly might get her stuck in between."

"She's right. But I think I know how to figure out which

vampire it was," I said, fetching the broom to start cleaning up the salt before Ichabod could make a bigger mess.

"How?" Harlow asked, settling on the couch to contain the wild beast that had broken our circle.

All three of them looked at me as I smiled. "I'm going to need yarn."

16
RAMONA

I wandered into Black Cat Knit Shop a little after noon, a tune on my lips. I was still feeling at ease after the collection of the succubus's soul a few nights prior. I'd been holed up in my house, attempting to detox my senses of a certain witch. I told myself that it had worked, but that was before I'd stepped onto the streets of Maple Hollow again. Now, I kept hallucinating a flash of red hair in my periphery . . . which, of course, I kept telling myself didn't mean anything.

With my worries finally few, I strolled through the rows of yarn and toward the gathering at the back of the shop.

"Ramona!" Agnes called from the knitting circle of vampires. "I was wondering when we'd see you back at knitting club."

It felt silly, but having the distraction of old acquaintances and local gossip felt like a much-needed comfort after everything that had happened. Especially when I was dangerously deficient in caffeine since I was avoiding the

café. And Midnight Market, the bakery, and the bookshop. All places I knew she frequented . . . or so I presumed.

I waved to Agnes and pulled my needles and yarn out of the only tote bag I owned. It was bloodred with my sigil emblazoned in gold on the front—my first embroidery project. No one could mistake it for theirs, so I wouldn't have to threaten anyone if my very rare and hard-to-source vicuña wool went missing. It was softer than cashmere and rarer than diamonds.

"You're just in time. Loraine was about to tell us about the run-in she had with an ogre a few weeks ago." Agnes chortled. "And we've got a newcomer to the group this week too."

The vampire pointed the blunt ends of her onyx needles across the circle right as Edith shifted back in her seat, revealing none other than Iris, who sat gnashing her knitting needles together, unaware of how badly she was mangling whatever mustard monstrosity she was attempting to make.

"Lucifer, fucking save me," I muttered.

"I didn't know you were a part of the knitting club," she said when I sat in the only available chair.

Which happened to be next to hers.

I curled my lip back. "I have hobbies," I muttered back, taking out my current project, which at present was only a navy-blue sleeve.

"Like rescuing stray cats and volunteering with the elderly?" Iris whispered back. "You make fun of me for my sweater vests while you're secretly part of a vampire knitting circle? Hello, pot. I'm kettle."

"How did you know I was going to be here?" I murmured from the corner of my mouth. "Are you stalking me?"

The vampires chattered amongst themselves about their favorite local feeding grounds—apparently, the dumpster behind the police station was the place to be these days. On the menu had been a blend of rowdy locals who'd crossed one of them at the market and tourists who hadn't respected the sanctity of Bones and Tomes or Ghoulish Antiques.

All young men, unsurprisingly—who'd been trying to peacock for townies who would rather eat them than sleep with them.

"I have better things to do with my time than try and follow your grumpy self around town," Iris replied. "This is just a pleasant surprise."

"Grumpy?" My frown deepened as I started working on my project.

I'd finally started feeling like I had this situation under control, like I wasn't seeing Iris's face every time I closed my eyes. But of course, she'd had to show up here and ignite my nerves like a live wire in a lightning storm. Whatever delusions I had about my nonexistent feelings for her were ruined by her presence.

I kept my expression a steely neutral. "You developed a sudden penchant for knitting?"

Her shoulder lifted and fell. "I have a lead."

She was pleased with herself. I could hear it in her tone.

I cursed as I dropped a stitch. "I thought I told you to—"

"Yeah, well, you should've known I wouldn't listen," she snapped back, looking up at me with those big green eyes, her lips pinched like the fucking brat she was.

I thought of all the ways I'd enjoy punishing her for her mouthy retorts. When I finally called in her debt, neither heaven nor hell was going to stop me from making her howl my name louder than a hell beast.

Fuck, Ramona. Get your head straight.

I narrowed my eyes. "You suspect vampires?"

"Mm-hmm."

"What is it we're being accused of now?" Avery, Agnes's daughter, shot daggers at us from her sharply winged eyes. "Yet another thing you demons are placing on the vampires?"

"Not at knitting club, kids," Agnes chided.

Only the *click-clack* of knitting needles filled the room for a tense moment. Demons and vampires had been at odds for centuries. Since around the fall of Rome, to be more specific. Once the Catholic church had taken hold of Europe and had begun spreading Catholicism to every corner of the world, vampires and demons had become targets. At times, it was more convenient to let vampires take the fall for certain demonic escapades. Only tentative truces kept us from turning on each other.

"No demon is crossing the treaty," I assured Avery, but gestured toward Iris. "It's the witch who has brought a question to the table. Nothing more than a question."

Avery eyed Iris, and the hunger in her gloomy grey eyes stoked the possessive fire I had been trying to smother.

"Don't be shy." Agnes sounded cheerier than I expected. "There are no secrets at knitting club."

I should have let Iris answer, but Avery looked murderous. "Agnes," I said, appealing to the good sense of my friend, "is there any chance there's a new vampire in town? One who may not understand the dynamics of our delicate ecosystem?"

"Not that I know of," Agnes replied, her thin, snowy brow lifting. "And I know everything."

"Any of your ilk stepping out of line lately?" Iris piped up next to me. "Anyone going through a rebellious phase?"

Agnes pursed her lips. "When are we not rebellious?" She let out a watery laugh. "But no, nothing against town ordinances or ancient treaties."

"That's both a relief and disheartening," I admitted. "I've been the target of some . . . unsavory evil."

Every eye in the circle was on me. It was rare for a demon to admit they were in trouble, and even rarer that they asked for help.

"I'm sorry to hear that, Ramona." Agnes refocused on the shawl she was knitting. "I hope this doesn't dampen your passion for good gossip and fashion patterns."

"Was it in town?" Avery asked. "Or a town nearby?"

"Why would that matter?" Agnes asked.

Avery cringed. "I didn't think it was worth mentioning. She knows she can't come back to Maple Hollow. The vampires all forbade her from returning."

My gut clenched.

I silently prayed to Satan, Beelzebub, Mammon, and every other king of hell that it wasn't who I thought it was. "Who?"

"Esme," Avery answered.

At those two syllables, I wished the floor would open up and swallow me whole.

"A vampire named Esme? Real original." Iris snorted. "I've never heard of a vampire by that name in Maple Hollow before."

But I could barely hear her over my roaring pulse. I snapped my knitting needle in two, nerves mounting with each passing second. Suddenly, it all made sense. "I thought she started a new coven out west?"

"As far as we all knew, she did," Avery replied. "But I bet all that rain in Washington gets tiring, even for the damned. You know how that goes, don't you, demon?"

"Let me get this straight. There's a vampire named Esme who moved to the Pacific Northwest and started a coven?" Iris cackled. "Goddess, I can't wait to tell Jordyn about this."

"I'm not sure why the little witch is so amused," Margret squeaked from across the circle. "This is a serious matter, Avery, you should have told us."

"She was always nice to me." Avery's resolve started to wane now that everyone was looking at her for answers. "I've only seen her once, and it was for less than five minutes."

Iris's head swiveled from one member of the group to another, her smile long gone by the time she landed on my harried expression. "Is she really that bad?"

"If ever there was a personification of an unpredictable rogue, it would be Esme," Agnes said with a shake of her head. "She wasn't made for discreet. She was a part of our coterie for about half a century before she became bored. Then she became a liability." She tipped her head at me and then looked back at Iris. "The two of them used to be thick as thieves once upon a time."

"Oh really?" Iris asked.

"It was mutual boredom, nothing more," I corrected. "She and I had a friendly rivalry going for a few centuries. Demon versus vampire, trying to see who could lure a soul into darkness first." I held Iris's gaze, imploring her to hear me. "We did a lot of terrible things together. She's incredibly dangerous."

If I couldn't convince myself to stay away from Iris, then perhaps I'd need to convince her to stay away from me. Things never ended well for me in friendship or romance. I needed to end whatever was going on between us before it actually began. Unfortunately, Iris didn't seem the least bit cowed.

"You two were the talk of the town back then," Agnes said with an approving nod. "Alas, Esme wasn't particularly careful with her feeding habits. She didn't care that we had a steady supply of human blood without having to cover up mysterious disappearances. We had all agreed to only take what we needed to survive, relieve the humans of those specific memories, and allow them to live another day." Agnes shook her head. "But when the surrounding larger cities started to catch wind of more and more humans turning up dead from 'animal attacks,' there was hell to pay. A slayer came, and our house was raided. It was a blood-bath, and not the kind we like to indulge in."

"When was this?" Iris's fingers tightened on her knitting needles.

"Back in the nineties," Agnes answered. "Some teen on a *Buffy* kick. We lost some of our oldest vampires that day. Those of us who did survive had to act. So with the witches' help, we banished Esme from Maple Hollow, and she moved on without a formal goodbye. Rumors and obituaries indicated a trail out toward Portland and the forests of the Pacific Northwest."

"But you don't know that this is necessarily her," Avery cut in, and I scrutinized the young vampire. "How could she even do anything to you, Ramona? You're too powerful."

"Oh, it's her," I said, rising to stand. Everything was suddenly clicking into place. "My most coveted possessions start to go missing with advanced magic around the same time you claim to have seen her? I don't believe in coincidences, especially ones so obvious."

"Does this Esme have wavy brown hair and blue eyes?" Iris asked.

I whirled toward her. "How do you know that?"

Iris winced. "I summoned one of your missing souls last night."

"You what?" I growled.

Her cheeks reddened. "I told you I had a lead. Maude said someone with long teeth visited her right before she died."

"Maybe it is handy to have a witch in the knitting circle," Agnes said with a mischievous lilt. "You sure are lucky she's on your side, Ramona."

"I don't have time for this," I snarled, stuffing my knitting project back into my bag. "I need to go find her."

Iris leaped to her feet. "I can—"

"You are *not* coming with me, witchling," I seethed. "You've put yourself in enough danger as it is. Go warn your coven. Then go home and *stay there*."

I didn't look back. I couldn't. The blind rage filling my vision was only meant to be seen by the person who truly deserved it.

Esme.

After all this time, I couldn't believe she'd come back.

17
IRIS

Ow dare she get mad at me for giving her a lead! If I hadn't summoned Maude, if I hadn't pushed Avery for answers, if I hadn't injected myself where I didn't belong, Ramona would've been royally fucked. She should've been kissing my ass instead of ordering me around like I was a foolhardy witchling. One day she'd realize how valuable I was and then she'd be sorry. *Yeah, Iris, that'll be the day.*

I stood outside the knit shop, fuming, both unwilling to storm after Ramona and unwilling to go home after being ordered to return there by the storm cloud that called herself a demon. Agnes and the vampires didn't know where Esme was, but someone else might. There was still more to be done, more that I could've helped with if Ramona had cared to ask. I needed to find someone who knew when people moved in and out of town.

I took out my phone and called Jordyn.

She answered on the first ring. "Hey! How did it go in the

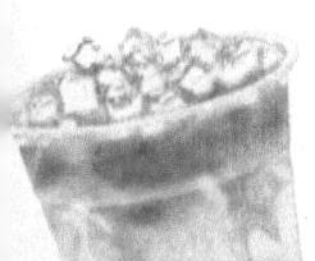

knitting circle? Did they *actually* knit or just talk about bloodsucking?"

"I'll tell you later," I cut in. "I'm headed to Midnight Market. Will you be at the apartment later? I'll catch you up then." I'd already started walking, weaving through the crowds that drifted in waves through the town square.

"Sounds good," Jordyn replied. "I'm finishing up inventory, then helping Harlow close up the café. But after that, we'll be here." The sounds of clanking glasses in the background stopped, and the chime of the bell above the door rang. The sound muffled as I suspected Jordyn held her phone against her sweater before calling out, "Welcome to the Poison Apple Apothecary! I'll be with you in a moment." More muffling, then she said in a low voice, "Call me if you need backup, okay?"

"I will. Bye."

"Bye."

A large warehouse of a building, Midnight Market was a one-stop shop for tourists, housing everything from spooky gift shops to local artisanal foods. The ice cream kiosk was the first stall inside, and that was where I knew I'd find our mayor—and hopefully another lead on my ill-advised case.

As I got closer, I could see families filtering in and out of the market area. The flower shop must have been having a sale because many tourists were leaving with large bouquets of sunflowers, strawflowers, and bright orange roses nested in sprigs of colorful leaves, all tied with big gingham bows as if they were all winners at the county fair.

Smiling children with purple-and-black swirl cotton candy as big as their heads followed their parents from the market and into the town square, where some locals were setting up booths for the night's bonfire. Rudy was already setting up the cider stand as Randy warmed the barrels. The police chief, Dougall, was moonlighting at the s'mores stand, sharpening sticks with his whittling knife. Eloise waved to me as she strung up twinkling lights around the witch-hat gazebo while Agnes rushed across the lawn, carrying a wicker basket filled with woolen scarves that I assumed she'd knitted herself. The town was in full swing. And despite most citizens being curmudgeonly magical creatures, I knew they secretly loved this time of year. They couldn't quite contain their enthusiasm as they all pitched in.

I sighed, breathing in the scent of wood fire and the slight chill in the air before heading indoors. Inside, Midnight Market was bustling. Customers circulated at every vendor, and the main walkways separating the shops were packed with meandering window shoppers. I squeezed through the crowd and slipped into the ice cream shop, ready to interrogate Billy, only to find a new face manning the line.

"Welcome to Midnight Market," said the tall green monster in a black paper hat as he handed an orange plastic spoon with chocolate ice cream to the woman at the front of the line. "Here is your sample, ma'am."

His thick stitched arm stretched over the glass top of the ice cream fridge and placed it into the woman's waiting fingers. She quickly stuck it in her mouth and giggled.

This—I assumed—was Billy's nephew, Dean. I could see now why Citrine had blushed a deep shade of crimson when she'd spoken of him. He was a Calvin Klein version of Frankenstein's monster: ripped, chiseled, and handsome. Albeit green.

Even the human customers seemed enamored with him.

Each person ahead of me in line tried sample after sample, but the monster only smiled and obliged.

"Here's my number," one woman said, sliding a scrap of paper across the ice cream freezer glass. "If you want to catch up after you take that stage makeup off tonight."

I had to bite the inside of my cheek to keep from laughing. She was bold. I'd give her that. Little did she know that the "stage makeup" she was referring to was his actual skin.

But Dean was a natural and simply said, "Unfortunately, I have a girlfriend." He took the paper and dropped it in the trash can beside him. "But how about a scoop of our *Hocus Pocus* Pistachio on the house?"

She tittered something unintelligible and nodded.

Damn, Dean. He was going to give Randy a run for his money as the town's boy-toy.

When I finally reached the front of the long line, he gave me a bright smile. "What can I get for you today?"

"I was actually looking for Billy. Is he around?"

"He's on break but should be back any minute, sorry." He looked genuinely apologetic. I was about as straight as a corkscrew and he had me blushing. What kind of magic did this monster weave? "Care for a sample while you wait?"

"Ha! I mean. Sure. Um." After all, when was the last time I'd stopped into Midnight Market for a treat? "What's the most popular flavor this week?"

"The Pumpkin Cheesecake Swirl is my personal favorite," he answered with a wide grin of surprisingly white teeth. "It's a cheesecake base, with locally sourced milk from Dutchman's Dairy. The graham-flavored sponge cake is from Full Moon Bakery, and the swirl is a mix of green custard and chocolate cookies to represent the swamp. It looks gross but tastes delicious."

"Much like yourself, I'd bet," I murmured.

"What?"

"What?" I exclaimed. "I said I'd love a sample, thanks!"

"Oh, okay." He scooped out a sample larger than the others he gave out—which I really shouldn't have cared about—and handed it to me.

"Wow," I said when I sucked on the spoon. It really didn't sound like the flavors would work together, but it was delicious. "That's inventive. Sorry, what is your name?"

I already knew, but he didn't know that. Maybe I could get him talking.

"Dean," he replied, pointing to the name badge on his pinstripe apron. "I'm Billy's nephew. Sort of." He winked, and I knew that he meant he'd been created within Billy's family somehow, though I wasn't exactly sure how his particular species went about it.

"Nice to meet you, Dean. I'm Iris." I swept my hair behind my ear and hooked my thumb in the direction behind me. "I work over at the Poison Apple Apothecary. Welcome to town."

"You're one of the local witches." His smile widened as he scooped another sample and passed it to me with a flourish that made it look like I wasn't holding up the line. "In Citrine's coven?"

"Yup. That's the one." I made a mental note that he was just as giddy mentioning Citrine as she was about mentioning him. Maybe I would need to have my own little Cher Horowitz moment with those two. I took a bite of the new sample, and a rich, decadent flavor blossomed on my tongue. "Mmm, this is really good! What's this one?"

He beamed at me as if he'd churned it himself. "It's called Death by Chocolate."

"Hey there, Iris." Billy's gruff voice came from behind Dean. Our mayor was six four but seemed short compared to his nephew, though there was plenty of family resemblance despite the fact that Dean's people skills were silky smooth and Billy's were gravel sandpaper. "Grabbing some seasonal favorites, I see?"

Billy lifted an apron from the wall and slipped it over his mop of bedraggled black hair. Then he gave the checkout assistant a nod, which I assumed was a signal for them to take their break.

"I'll take one scoop of the Death by Chocolate, please," I said to Dean. I gave the tall, green glass of water a final once-over, scheming all the ways I could set him up with my coven sister, before moving down the line to Billy. "Hey, Billy? Could I ask you something about a resident who used to live here?"

Billy tilted his head at me, the stretch in his neck pulling at what looked like a new set of sutures. "I always have time for my constituents, no matter how unruly."

There was that winning mayoral charm.

I lowered my voice so that no one could overhear. "Do you know anything about someone named Esme?"

"Hmm, that sounds familiar." His thick brow furrowed. "Was she part of the local coven?"

"No," I replied. "Have you seen anyone around town with wavy brown hair and blue eyes?"

"That's not a lot to go off of. I think there are two people in line right now that fit that description."

"Never mind." I waved the thought away with a laugh.

He considered me for a moment, and something in my gut told me to keep any further information to myself. If word got back to Ramona that I was questioning local monsters out in broad twilight, it would be my head.

"Here's your cup." Dean held out an overflowing cup of ice cream.

"Thanks." I dug into my pocket, pulled out a five-dollar bill, and handed it to Billy. "Keep the change. Your new staff member is quite the salesman."

Billy clapped Dean on the shoulder. "The apple doesn't fall far from the tree."

I made my way out of the market, doing my best to avoid any figures lurking in the shadows. I didn't want to admit it, but Ramona was right. Esme could be anywhere, or worse, working with someone in town. And not knowing who meant I had to be more discreet. But the fact that Billy Bacchus hadn't seen her around was useful information—useful enough that maybe I needed to pay that stubborn demon a visit and tell her as much.

18

RAMONA

I was leaning against my kitchen island, staring mindlessly into space, when a loud banging sounded at my door. I rolled my eyes and pushed off and went to answer it. People banged on my door for all sorts of reasons. Hopefully, it was another wayward human looking to make a foolish deal.

I straightened my collar, grinning as I prowled closer. But when I opened it, Wyatt stood there, gasping for breath.

"What did you do?" he growled, pushing past me and stumbling into my house.

"What the hell happened to you?" I asked, taking in the state of him. "You look like you fell face-first into a dozen witches' brooms."

He staggered into the living room and knocked into the wall hard enough to cause my prized Rembrandt to drop to the floor, frame shattering. He had no idea what I'd gone through to get my hands on that. The piece had once hung in the Montreal Museum of Fine Art, but it had been in my

possession for over fifty years. That might have been my thieving chickens coming back to roost.

"Could you please refrain from destroying every priceless artifact in my home, wolf boy?" I followed him into the room as my frown deepened. "Heists aren't as easy to conduct as they used to be."

"You—" Before he could get the words out, he doubled over, gnashing his teeth.

"If you wolf out all over my furniture, I will be invoicing you," I warned. "And I don't take payment in the form of scones—or even your sister's famous donuts."

Wyatt groaned in either frustration or pain—I didn't know and didn't care—but as he turned around, I got a full view of the situation we were dealing with. He was shirtless, the tattered remnants of his flannel hanging from his wrists. His canines were elongated, his blond hair even shaggier than usual, and his voice was even deeper than normal, rough and rasping. His true animal nature was nearly bursting from his skin, the change almost taking him in my fucking living room.

The realization hit me like a rogue wave. *He shouldn't be in this state at all.*

"What the hell happened?" I asked again, but my question was answered when my eyes dropped to his collarbone.

His sigil—*my sigil*—was missing.

"Shit."

"Yeah, shit," he growled. "You said your magic was *binding*. You promised she—I would be safe." He took a long, thick pause. All of his visible muscles bulged, readying themselves for the change. But there was a twinge of mourning in his voice when he finally said, "If anything happened to her."

"To whom?"

He hung his head, swiping his disheveled hair out of his eyes. "Willow."

"Fuck." My eyes darted to the door as if I could see all the way to the café. "Is she hurt?"

"No," he gritted out like it pained him. "Not physically, at least."

I glared up at the ceiling. "It's the full moon, isn't it?"

"Yes." He sucked in sharp breaths in a seeming attempt to battle the shift.

"The fact you've controlled it this long is a fucking miracle. You need to get out of here," I pushed. "Besides, I just reupholstered my furniture, and the last thing I need is a werewolf humping it."

His luminescent eyes flared, and I was fairly certain he was about two seconds away from attacking me. What a terrible time to have a snarky sense of humor as a coping mechanism.

"Go. Shift," I added more evenly. "You won't survive like this. You need to change. Resisting it could kill you."

"I won't give in to them." His whole body shook like he was lifting an incredible weight, every muscle straining to keep him from losing control. "I won't give them what they want."

"Did you catch sight of who it was who broke the sigil?" I asked, teetering on the edge of the realization.

"Woman. Not human," he gritted out. "Supernatural. I tried to chase her, but she evaded me. Jumped me on the way to Willow's. Tried to fucking stab me. Thought it was a rogue ghoul, but that thing didn't know who it was trying to kill. It ran when I fought back. I didn't realize she'd broken the sigil until it was too late."

"Esme."

"Who?"

"A former friend," I replied tightly. "And current annoyance."

He let out a bellowing growl. "This isn't over, Ramona," he snarled. "You need to fix this. Or I will *end you*, demon. Don't take that threat lightly."

"I don't," I bit out.

Wyatt was next in line to be the alpha, unless he halted his ability to shift. And as much as he wanted to delay that reality, I didn't want to be on the wrong end of a would-be alpha and his pack. The werewolves would run me out of town if I didn't make this right.

And if I was out of town, I wouldn't be near Iris.

That shouldn't have been my first thought. That shouldn't have been *any* thought. But that fucking little redheaded witch was the first thing that flashed in my mind.

A sudden and terrible realization dawned on me: Esme wasn't just stealing my souls. She wouldn't have attacked Wyatt if she just wanted to break my sigil. No. She was *killing* my marks. Why else would she attack Wyatt instead of finding a more cunning way to break my sigil? I thought whoever was targeting my souls was toying with me, but this went beyond stealing debts. I should've known Esme would be more ruthless than that. And if she went after Wyatt, it would only be a matter of time before she went after—

"Iris." My cold, black heart sank into my stomach.

"What?" Wyatt sounded more animal than man.

His skin pulled tighter on his back as he turned tail and headed back down the hallway. Lucky for him, I lived on the edge of the haunted woods where he could change in peace, away from the eyes of his pack. I followed Wyatt to the front door, ready to charge into the night and find Iris. I already knew there was no way that little witch had heeded my warnings.

As he stumbled to the door, Wyatt's fingernails grew into claws and raked marks into my wallpaper. I didn't voice my objections, not with an almost-werewolf in my house, and instead ushered him to the door.

"You better catch the bitch who did this."

"Oh, believe me, I will," I said, giving him an assured nod. "Get to the deepest parts of the woods as fast as you can. It'll be safe for everyone if you get lost for a few hours."

He ran down the path from my entryway to the gate, practically barreling into none other than a wide-eyed Iris.

Relief coursed through me like a living thing.

She's here. She's safe.

The two of us watched as a shirtless Wyatt stormed to the end of the street and then disappeared into the shadows of the forest.

I folded my arms and leaned against the doorway, trying to mask the terror that was still heating my chest. "Just the witch I was looking for."

Iris had venom in her gaze, and all my feigned nonchalance evaporated. I straightened, wondering if she'd had a run-in with Esme too.

Iris flung her hand in the direction of the woods. "What was he doing here?"

"Huh?"

"Wyatt!" Her voice rose an octave. "Are you sleeping with him? Is that why Willow was upset the other night—"

"That's not—"

"I can't believe you fucked my best friend's girlfriend's sister's boyfriend!"

"One more degree and you'll get to Kevin Bacon." I winked, which only incensed her further.

"Why is Willow's boyfriend leaving your house half naked?"

"I didn't realize they'd made it official," I taunted. "I guess I missed that piece of town gossip."

She clenched her hands into fists. "I can't believe you."

A surprised smile stretched my lips. She was furious at me. A mix of satisfaction and glee mingled with the relief that she was here in front of me and not cornered somewhere by Esme. I normally liked getting this rise out of her, but this time, it was particularly savory.

"Jealousy looks so good on you, red," I purred.

"I'm *not* jealous," she spat.

"Of course not." I leaned back against the door, opening it farther. "But why don't you come in and lecture me more about it?"

Please, I thought. *I need you to be here, where you're safe and far, far away from whatever mess is happening with my other marks.*

"Are you kidding me?" She turned to leave, and my stomach dropped. "I think I'm going to be sick."

"Iris!" I called, stalling her. The sigil on Iris's collarbone was putting her in danger, and I wasn't about to let her out of my sight. "I would never sleep with Wyatt. Wolf boys are really not my type."

You're my type, I wanted to say, as if that weren't obvious.

"Then why was he half dressed and running out of your house?"

"It was Esme."

Her face was skeptical. "She's sleeping with Wyatt?"

"No. No one is sleeping with Wyatt." *That I know of.* I stalked down the path from my house. "Esme is out there hunting my marks. Which is why I need you to come inside and stay there until I've dealt with her." I closed the distance, brushing my fingertips to the *V* of her neckline and tracing over the raised brand on her skin.

"Why?" Iris asked breathlessly.

My eyes filled with heat as they met hers. "Because you're mine."

Even as she shuddered at my touch, she stepped away, shaking her head. She was stronger than I was in that regard. When it came to Iris, I knew I could lure her in but questioned whether I could keep her hooked. A flare of a challenge rose in me.

"I'll just keep the door locked at the apothecary," she said, clearing her throat.

I shook my head. "That welcome sign is invitation enough for a vampire. Who's to say she wasn't invited into the building long before you were even born."

"And she's never entered your house?"

"Never."

She stubbornly stuck out her lip. "I'll go stay with my family then."

"No."

"No?" she echoed in a mocking huff. "You don't get a say in what I do."

My pulse ratcheted up, the fear of her heading into danger so great that I panicked. I had to keep her here, by whatever means necessary.

She managed three more steps before I grabbed her by

the elbow and spun her around. My hand bracketed her jaw as I pulled her lips to mine and kissed her. She let out a little surprised sound that was so damn satisfying, but she didn't budge when my lips enveloped hers. Or when my tongue swept across her bottom lip, urging her to open for me.

"Stay here with me," I pleaded against her lips. "I promise to keep you deliciously occupied."

When she pulled away, there were tears in her eyes. "Pretending that you want me just to keep me here is low, even for you. Manipulating my feelings just so you don't lose another deal to your old rival—" She shook her head and staggered back a step.

Was that what she thought? Panic flared anew.

"That's not—"

What? What was I going to say? What was I willing to *admit* to her in that moment?

Nothing.

Nothing came out of my mouth.

I could promise her nothing. She and I had been doomed before we'd even begun. I wasn't made for someone as perfectly world changing as she was. And I certainly wasn't worthy of the way she looked at me. I was impossible to love, and I couldn't bear to see the moment when Iris realized that.

So instead of giving her a reason to stay, I just rocked back on my heels and watched as she whipped around and stormed into the night.

As soon as she trailed out of sight, I took out my phone to call in a favor from Naphula. Someone needed to guard the witch while I was hunting Esme. The phone rang and rang, neither going to voicemail nor picking up.

"Shit," I snarled. "Fucking useless."

I dialed the next number I could think of and was utterly relieved when a voice answered on the first ring. "Witch's Brew Café, this is Harlow."

19
IRIS

With swollen lips and bleary eyes, I darted through the town square, uncaring that I'd be the talk of the town for my dramatics. The tears that came thick and fast surprised me. I couldn't contain them even if I tried.

I could've forgiven Ramona for tricking me into staying, for luring me in with her deceptions. Hell, I could've forgiven her for throwing me over her shoulder and tying me to a chair just to keep me there. But kissing me like I was the air she breathed when I knew it was all a ploy had been cruel, even for a demon.

And what was worse was that I knew I had no right to be hurt by it. This was what demons did—toyed with their marks, played with them like a cat with their many mice. I'd dug this grave for myself. After all, *I* had been the one chasing after *her*, goading her at every turn, pestering her, even. I was just another soul addicted to her allure. But for some ungodly reason, I still thought that I was different. That maybe I was special to her. I wanted to be.

Fuck.

The thought left me reeling, and I nearly barreled into Agnes and Billy Bacchus as they chatted about the Halloween Festival decorations and the fact that everything was "too beige these days." They ignored me as I stumbled past them.

A single thought rang like a Klaxon through my mind: *I wanted to be special to a demon.*

Had someone poisoned my tea? Was a lock of my hair being burned in a hex right now? What was I thinking?

I swiped at my eyes as I crunched across the thick layer of golden leaves toward the apothecary. When I reached the front door, Jordyn and Harlow were already standing there. But instead of canoodling like they usually did, they were frantically pouring a line of salt across the threshold while Jordyn muttered incantations while sparks of magic emanated from her fingertips.

"What's going on?" I called out.

Jordyn gave me a look that meant she was serious. "Get inside, quickly."

I dashed into the darkened apothecary.

"There." Jordyn shut the door and bolted it. "That should hold for at least a couple of hours before we have to start the ritual all over again."

Together, we ascended the stairs up to our apartment. Neither Jordyn nor I had been around much to clean, and we were greeted by sprawling clutter when we entered. Spell books were piled up on the coffee table, kitchen counter, and small dining table. Discarded teacups crowded the kitchen sink. Baskets of dried herbs and hastily discarded sweaters covered the couch.

"An extra-strength warding spell?" I asked incredulously. "What big bad has shown up in Maple Hollow this time?"

"Uh, hello! There's a rogue vampire on the loose, Iris!" Jordyn balked, grabbing me and pulling me into a fierce hug even as she chastised me.

"Oh, right. That," I muttered. "Does the whole town know?"

Ichabod mewed from his bed on the windowsill, which was crowded with candles and crystals.

"Ramona called the café," Harlow supplied, crossing the room and picking up our furry familiar. "She sounded furious."

My mouth fell open. "She *called the café?*"

"She said that Wyatt had been attacked by a vampire. And that you stormed off and that we needed to make sure you're safe and, if at all possible, convince you to go back to her house, which is probably the safest place in Maple Hollow to be right now, apparently."

"I am not going back!" I erupted. "Not after she—she kissed me."

"I knew it!" Harlow snapped, pointing a finger at a shocked Jordyn. "Told you."

"You don't seem particularly happy about this kiss," Jordyn hedged. "Talk to us. Harlow brought coffee and sugar cookies to hold us over for the evening."

"They're meant to be shaped like broomsticks, but they snapped in the cabinet," Harlow supplied. "We couldn't sell them at the café, but they still taste good. We really need to think of sturdier, more reliably shaped objects, like pumpkins."

"You've got a lot to catch us up on." Jordyn pulled me toward the couch and handed me a cookie. "Now, spill."

At first, I wavered on how much I should tell them. Tears pricked my eyes as I connected all the dots for them: the knitting circle discovery after the summoning, the stop at Midnight Market, and Wyatt leaving Ramona's house shirtless. Then I had to give them all the juicy details of the kiss Ramona and I had shared at the summer camp, all the way to Ramona's kiss less than an hour ago. When I finished, Jordyn stared at me for a long moment, her pinched mouth tight as if holding back her storming thoughts.

I folded my arms with a huff. "Whatever you're going to say, I've probably told myself the same thing a million times over."

Jordyn chuckled. "Are you sure? It may be exactly what you need to hear."

"Ugh, fine, tell me."

"I think you should go back to Ramona's," Jordyn said.

I nearly spat out my lukewarm latte. "Are you crazy?"

"If Esme is willing to go after a full-grown werewolf, then she'll have no qualms with attacking you."

"I agree," Harlow chimed in. "It may be awkward, but Ramona clearly wants to protect you."

"So she kissed you? So what?" Jordyn admonished.

"I can't believe you, the one who made me promise no demons, is saying this," I shot back.

"Things have changed," Jordyn countered. "I mean, sure, she's a terrifying hell dweller whose sole purpose on this plane is to entice unsuspecting people into giving her their souls, but who doesn't have baggage? You are still safer with her until this vampire is found."

"I'm safe here at home with you guys."

"No, you're not," Jordyn chided. "All we know about this vampire is that she used to live in Maple Hollow and she has it out for Ramona. We don't know how powerful she is or what access she was granted to one of these centuries-old buildings. Our warding spells are like flypaper. She'd have to step right into one of them for it to work, and we have no clue how long they'd hold. Vampires are tricky, and our kind of magic doesn't always work on them. You know that."

Ichabod meowed as if in agreement.

Just like him to take her side.

My shoulders drooped, and I let out a soft grunt of acknowledgment.

"Ramona's house is all shiny and new, which means it was built *after* Esme was banished," Jordyn continued. "Esme has never been welcomed across the threshold, and I stand to bet that Ramona would slit Esme's throat before she let her anywhere near you. You'll be safe with her."

"I don't know," I protested. "Agnes is a pretty powerful vampire, and Harlow nearly killed her with a rogue chai latte last year."

"It was a cappuccino," Harlow corrected with a glare.

"Still! I'll just dash some cinnamon at her! We have tons downstairs."

"Nutmeg!" Harlow threw her hands up. "And can we just move on from that? Agnes had the allergy in life and it followed her into her transformation as a vampire—I looked it up. So, who knows if crop-dusting Esme with a spice cabinet will even work?"

Jordyn gave Harlow a pat on the knee before turning back to me. "Listen, if you're adamant about staying here, we can figure it out." She looked exhausted just thinking of what that would entail. "I will call the coven and we'll take shifts all night patrolling for vamps on the prowl and recasting—"

"Don't call the coven," I cut in. "The last thing I need is getting my parents involved in this. And there will be more than hell to pay if the coven finds out that I made a deal with Ramona. We can't do that."

It was hard enough keeping the sigil and the true impact of my deal with Ramona from Jordyn; my parents would be so disappointed. I knew the secrets would come out eventually, just like Jordyn's had last year, but for now, the coven was safer not being involved. If Esme was as dangerous as Ramona insisted, there really was only one solution.

"I don't see any other way to keep you safe," Jordyn added more gently. "And I realize how hypocritical this is. I didn't want you anywhere near the demon. But what else can we do? Go stay with Ramona, we'll help hunt down this vampire, and then we can go back to life as usual."

I mindlessly stroked the sigil on my collarbone. The truth was, I didn't want to go back to life as usual. I wanted there to be a time when Ramona didn't need a sigil to want to kiss me, a time when she wanted me to be hers without making a deal.

Goddess, help me.

Going back to Ramona's house for protection felt like putting my feet directly to the fire. I didn't know if I could see her again without my heart breaking into a thousand pieces. I wanted us to be . . . *more* than a deal. And that thought just might kill me.

20

RAMONA

I stormed through the twilight streets, unsure of which way to turn. All I knew was that Esme was hiding somewhere in plain sight. That fucking bitch. She seemed to be around every corner and a mile ahead of me at the same time.

Only rage guided me. Rage at Esme, yes, but also at myself. I couldn't resist Iris's lips, and now they'd damned me worse than hell ever could. I should've just told her. Told her I liked my sigil on her skin, not like a collar around her neck but like a ring on her finger. That I was just as drawn to her as she was to me. That we belonged to each other, connected through magic, yes, but also something more.

But I wasn't a sentimental sap, or at least I shouldn't be. I didn't have the words to tell her I wanted her, that despite pushing her away, it thrilled me every time she stubbornly appeared again. The truth was it terrified me—*she* terrified me. I could deal with monsters and ghosts, but the way I felt about this girl was scarier than anything this paranormal town had to offer.

"Dammit!" I gritted out, punching the unyielding brick beside me.

"You've always had such a fiery temper," a familiar voice crooned. "You should really work on that, darling."

I whirled, saying her name before my eyes even landed on her. "Esme."

"Hello, old friend. Miss me?"

I found her standing just inside the threshold of the broomstick shop. Her pale skin shimmered in the dwindling light of the sunset. Wavy brown curls framed her round face and made her normally blue eyes shimmer bronze with hunger. She was always the bronze to my silver, always one step behind me. And this time, it was no different. Whatever game she was playing would end with her head separated from her body, her ashes scattered far from Maple Hollow. Far from Iris.

Ready to throttle her, I stormed toward the doorway but crashed to a halt as I collided with a hard wall of air. The unseen barrier pulsed against my palm as if alive and laughing at me.

"Warding the broomstick shop against me *before* taunting me? You always were spineless."

Esme pursed her lips, tilting her head from side to side. "I just wanted to give you a little taste of what I'm working with these days, old friend. Wards are just one of the many little witch tricks I picked up on my travels."

I hated how kept she looked. Wherever she'd been hiding clearly hadn't been unpleasant. Usually, lone vampires lost their sanity after a few solitary months. I knew she had found a new brood of vamps out in Washington, but had she brought them back with her? Someone would have noticed a whole new nest of vampires skulking around, right?

"Demons are so easy to ward against." Esme flashed a devilish smile, her fangs glinting in the streetlights that had been triggered by the sinking sun. "I've actually been able to ward a few other town shops from you and any other demons."

She started counting off on her long, slim fingers. "Midnight Market, Stars and Stones, Black Cat Knit Shop . . ." Her eyes pinned me through the veil she'd created. "The Poison Apple Apothecary."

My fist slammed into the hard force field as I let out a feral growl. My knuckles split, but I ignored the pain even as blood dripped down my fingertips. "I swear to Lucifer, Esme, if you hurt her . . ."

"I guess I finally found the weak link in your armor." Esme's smile widened. "You always did have a thing for the cute, little artsy ones."

I curled my lip. "I'm going to enjoy killing you. Step outside and fight me, you coward."

She threw her head back and cackled. "Now, what sort of fun would that be? Ending the game so soon after I've spent so much time preparing it for you?"

"You're the only one playing games," I growled. "Why are you doing this?"

She shrugged. "Fifty years is an awfully long time in human years. But I was there when you offered Saul that deal, don't you remember? I knew his time was just about up. And what a perfect time for a little visit."

"I won that coin toss fair and square. My deal or your fangs. Smarter heads won out."

Saul had been miserable all those years ago. The deal I

provided, he'd realized, didn't solve his issues and had been a fate worse than death by fangs. But he'd gotten what he'd wished for: a long life safe from monsters and an astoundingly successful business, to boot.

"Come on, Ro." She pushed her bottom lip out in an exaggerated pout. "We used to get up to all sorts of mischief. Don't you miss it?"

"No, I don't. Just tell me what you want so we can get to the part where I paint the town red with your blood."

"There's that fire that always made men quake in their boots." There was a crazed glint in her eyes. "My feisty counterpart."

Esme had always been anarchic and unpredictable, but this deranged state was new. We'd spent years gallivanting together, doing the most wicked deeds just for the simple pleasure of them, but she'd never turned against me like this.

"You know I don't need a reason," Esme said as if reading my mind. "Though, I suppose some would say that you letting me get run out of town was reason enough. A true friend would have stood up for me, or at least come with me on a new adventure."

"You were reckless and refused to cover your tracks. Which brought the slayer here! There was nothing I could have done to stop them."

"But you stayed!" Her eyes widened and her voice pitched to a new height, shattering the illusion of indifference.

"Demons have no need to go on the run. I was building a stronghold here, and staying was the right choice."

"You became slow and boring," she pushed. "You'd rather craft handmade holiday cards than kill for the fun of it anymore. What kind of demon are you? No." She shook her head. "This town ruined you, Ramona, and instead of coming out west with me, you tossed me aside like trash."

"This is pointless." I pinched the bridge of my nose. "Tell me what I need to do to get you to leave."

"Entertain me," Esme said with a delighted grin. "Play my little game of cat and mouse."

This had always been her problem. She would make terrible choices just because she could, get us into terrible scrapes, and then I'd have to dig us out of trouble. She was the worst kind of friend. I should've known she'd come back to haunt me.

"You set up this senseless game of stealing my souls to what? Best me?" I glared at her. "How is that any fun for you?"

"Oh, I'm having a ball," she purred. "You should've seen your face when you discovered old Saul. You didn't even think to look around you before you left, storming out like a raincloud. I think that little witch of yours has distracted you for far longer than I've been back. How about you tell me all about her. Iris, right? Such a pretty little thing."

"You do *not* touch her," I growled, more feral than a werewolf now. "She is *mine*."

Esme yawned, attempting to seem bored. "She won't be for long. I know how to break your claim on her." Her eyes panned down my body, sizing me up. "Do you think she'll still be so enamored with you after your sigil is broken? She won't owe you anything. Will she still follow you around like a lost puppy when she isn't compelled to by your magic?"

A new wave of hatred filled my chest. Esme's smile widened as her words struck true, just as she'd clearly planned. I was well versed in concealing my temper, but Esme had known me too well for too long.

"Why would someone as vibrant as she is want someone as dead inside as you?" She shook her head at me. "Look at you. Becoming blander by the day, turning into a sad, pathetic version of the demon you once were. You used to be mighty, Ramona. But this town has made you soft."

"I like this town. I like who I am here. And so does Iris," I said like I was trying to convince myself.

The way Iris had looked at me, the hurt in her eyes . . .

There was something there if I were only brave enough to grab it.

"You needed a reckoning, Ramona." Esme clicked her tongue, pulling me from that thought. "I'm that reckoning."

"Esme—"

She turned halfway toward the shadowy shop. "I'll make you a deal." She examined her ruby-red nails. "I'll give you a few days to think it over to be a good sport. If you agree to come with me and give up this embarrassing, kitschy town, I'll let the witch live."

I didn't have to think about it, but I did need time. We both knew I'd do anything, but still I said, "And if I don't agree?"

"Then the game isn't over." Esme shrugged and the door magically shut in my face.

21

IRIS

I sat on the stoop of Ramona's house, Jordyn and Harlow flanking me like guard dogs. I rubbed my arms, wishing I had brought a thicker coat. We'd hit the sudden temperature dip as late October approached. If we hadn't been waiting for over an hour, I might've still had feeling in my toes. Though, we had confirmed that knocking on her door or ringing her doorbell wouldn't summon her from thin air like we'd previously assumed.

When Ramona finally did return, she was so lost in her own thoughts that she didn't even notice us waiting until she was halfway up the path to her front door. She wore a steely expression and looked pristine as ever, apart from one bloodied hand that hung limply by her side.

I sucked in a little breath at the sight of the blood, unsure if it was hers or someone else's. The sound made Ramona lift her head, her eyes landing directly upon mine, and when they did, her rigid posture visibly crumpled in relief.

"You going to be okay?" Jordyn murmured as Ramona strode up the walkway toward me.

"Yeah." I hugged my friend as I stood, my ass numb from sitting on the cold stone for so long.

Harlow gave me a quick hug, too, before turning toward Ramona and making an "I'm watching you" gesture. Then Harlow slung an arm around Jordyn's shoulders and my friends walked into the night.

I chuckled at the boldness of my chivalrous human friend. There was no way that she could take on a powerful demon, but with her loyalty and stubbornness, I knew she'd try.

Ramona gave a bemused look at Harlow as they crossed paths before coming to a stop at the stoop.

"You came back," she finally stated, her expression unreadable.

"I did," I replied, nervously sweeping a lock of hair behind my ear. "You're hurt." I reached for her hand, and she indulged me as I inspected her split knuckles.

"You should see the other guy," she said with a groan as I pressed a finger to the wound. "What are you—"

"Let me fix it," I insisted, holding my fingers over her hand as magic swirled from my fingertips. "Hold still."

For once, she listened.

I whispered a healing incantation, and her wounds closed over to fresh skin, still pink and a little swollen but nearly healed.

"I could've done that myself, you know," she murmured.

"I know." I realized I was still holding her hand. Her fingers slowly splayed to encircle my wrist, but I nervously pulled away from her touch. "I just, uh, wanted to help."

"Thank you." She cleared her throat, putting her hands in her pockets as if putting them in timeout.

"Are you going to tell me what happened, or do I need to tap into my clairvoyance?" I put my hands on my hips for effect, but there was no bite. She didn't owe me an explanation after I'd stormed off only to sheepishly return for her protection.

"You're full of surprises." She smiled down at me, but worry and sadness were in her eyes. "I had no idea you were clairvoyant."

The blush on my cheeks gave me away in an instant. "Technically, I'm not, but I could make a few calls to the rumor mill and figure it out pretty quick."

"Ah, so you'd use your witchy wiles for information, then?"

Her shoulders relaxed, and the tension in my own melted too.

"My wiles have to be good for something."

She huffed a laugh, and we slipped into silence.

I looked all around me—the streetlights, the twinkling stars, the garden gate—but all I saw was that molten kiss that was burned into the back of my mind. My gaze lingered on her stoop, which was decorated with fall flowers and an expertly carved jack-o'-lantern of a witch flying on a broomstick, a crescent moon behind her.

"Wow. Who did you get that from?" It was an awkwardly executed attempt to carry on the conversation. "Randy?"

"I made it, actually."

"You made *that*? The *Mona Lisa* of pumpkins?"

She just shrugged. "I told you I had hobbies." She

swirled her fingers and the locked door behind me opened. "Come on. I have something I want to show you."

I warily followed her inside. "Please tell me it isn't some poor soul strung up on a rack wearing its intestines as a necklace."

Her chuckle was deep and rasping. "I mean, I do collect antique torture devices," she teased. "But what I want to show you is in the kitchen."

"Heads in jars?"

She glanced over her shoulder at me. "That's more of a witch thing." She winked and my stomach flipped.

Shit.

Maybe I should've made Jordyn and Harlow stay with me. If Ramona winked at me like that again, I thought my panties would combust of their own volition.

With a shaky breath, I followed her down a long, dark hallway without a single decoration on the walls, apart from a lone nail that I guessed once held artwork. The first two rooms were austere and cold, with steel and black furnishings like some neo-modern city loft, but when we poured out into the kitchen, I caught little notes of personality—warmth, even: a scented candle, an embroidered tea towel, a ceramic bowl of crystals, and a floral painting reminiscent enough of Georgia O'Keefe to make clear that this was a sapphic home.

"I'll be honest, I was expecting more damned souls and fewer vulva flowers."

Ramona didn't miss a beat. "The kitchen felt like the most appropriate place for the painting."

"Why?"

"Isn't that what people do in kitchens?" Her silver eyes

met mine. "Surround themselves with their favorite things to eat?"

I choked on my own air, a furious blush burning across my cheeks as I thought about just how skilled Ramona would be with her mouth . . .

A wicked smile stretched across Ramona's lips, as if she knew the exact image I was conjuring in my mind.

"Sit," she commanded.

If only she meant on her face, but instead, she gestured to a black leather bar stool.

As she navigated to the other side of the kitchen island, the distance cooled my burning cheeks. I really needed to pull myself together, but this demon seemed to know exactly what she was doing to me.

She opened the cabinet below the sink, pulled out a stack of newspapers, and slapped two serrated knives on top.

"Oh great, you're going to kill me," I muttered. "Just when I thought we were getting along."

Ramona let out an incredulous little huff as she bent down to the cabinet again and produced two basketball-sized pumpkins. "I need a few more to decorate the stoop. They look better in groups of three. Agnes has won the best Halloween porch for the last four years, and it's about time the old bat has her streak broken."

My nerves eased as I laughed. "Aspirations of brokering souls and winning the Maple Hollow best porch ribbons . . ."

"I'm a complicated demon."

Ramona set up two workstations, then gave me a pencil to sketch out my carving before she turned toward the stove.

"Is this your way of keeping me distracted?" I asked.

"Yes," she admitted, "but I needed something to keep

me busy too. Wyatt messaged. He's caught Esme's scent on the outskirts of town, and Agnes has the vamps on the prowl. Esme warded half the town against me, so I have to rely on the locals who also have a vested interest in her capture." I could tell she hated the fact that she had to depend on others and couldn't just do it herself. "But until they turn Esme to dust, we might as well do some crafting."

Ramona set a small saucepan on the stove and started whisking some milk. I watched with curiosity, my attention oscillating between my pumpkin and whatever brew she was concocting.

"At least this is a more honest way of luring me in than a kiss," I murmured, more to myself than to her.

With her back still to me as she stirred some dark powder into the mixture, Ramona said, "I didn't kiss you to keep you here."

"Oh?" *Goddess curse you, Iris! You suck at nonchalance!*

"Well, I did, but that wasn't the only reason," she added hastily, sprinkling other things into her mixture.

My mouth went drier than desert sand. "Oh."

"I kissed you because I wanted to," she said. "Simple as that. I kissed you because every time your lips leave mine, all I can think about is when we'll be joined again."

Fuck, fuck, fuck, Iris, say something more than "Oh!"

But I had no idea what to say. For once, I was completely tongue-tied. I was supposed to be good at this! But Ramona made me completely unhinged.

So, I swiveled my pumpkin around, half smiling, half cringing. "What do you think?"

What the fuck are you talking about! Stop it!

The demon peeked over her shoulder with a wicked

smile at my flustered expression. "Classic jack-o'-lantern," she said. "I approve."

"Cool."

Cool? Cool?!

I'm supposed to be good at this! How many women do I have to date before I stop acting like a giddy eighth grader with her first crush?

Goddess, why couldn't I just like men? They're so simple.

"You know," I added, trying to quell my rising nerves. *Yes, good. Words. Say something more intelligent now, please.* "For a witch who lives in a Halloween-themed town, I think I've only carved pumpkins once as a kid."

"I know what you mean." Ramona's head bobbed. "Sometimes, it feels like apple picking and pumpkin-carving are just touristy things around here. Not for the locals."

"Exactly."

"Here." She slid a steaming mug across the countertop.

I looked down at what appeared to be hot chocolate with a dollop of freshly whipped cream on top and a dusting of chocolate flakes.

My mouth instantly started salivating.

"Holy cow," was all I could say. "Thank you."

I took a sip, rich flavors alighting on my tongue. It was the perfect blend of sweet and spicy, the chocolate rich and decadent, the milk thick and creamy . . .

Was it possible to orgasm just from taste alone?

I let out a moan, and Ramona cleared her throat, shifting her weight at the sound, and I hoped she was as turned on as I was because, fuck, this hot chocolate might've been the best foreplay ever.

Well played, demon.

"Where did you learn to make this?"

With a pleased smile, Ramona replied, "I got the recipe from an elf in that Christmas town north of here . . ." She searched the ceiling as if trying to think of the name.

"Sugarplum Valley?" I supplied.

She snapped her fingers. "That's the one." Her hunter's eyes watched me as I took another sip.

"You're not having one?"

"Hell is plenty hot enough, love," she said with another panty-dropping wink. "I only drink cold drinks."

She turned and fetched a cold brew coffee from the fridge, pouring some of the leftover hot chocolate into it along with a heaping serving of dark ice cubes that I suspected were more frozen coffee. With her drink in hand, she rounded the kitchen island. She perched on a bar stool beside me and assessed her untouched pumpkin.

"Trying to figure out how to create stained glass for a Notre-Dame design?" I teased.

"Oh please, Gothic churches was last year's theme."

I snickered into my mug, the hot steam tickling the tip of my nose. "I think I'll keep the stoop on-theme and do some potion bottles."

"Sounds like a winner."

Leaning back in my stool, I sipped my hot chocolate and enjoyed the view of Ramona deep in concentration. She deftly prepped her canvas, and my stomach flipped once or twice at how her nimble fingers expertly carved and etched the pumpkin's thick orange flesh.

Of all the things that would turn me on . . . this was probably the most bizarre. But when it came to Ramona, everything seemed to turn me on.

And I would never admit it to her, but my panties were as wet as the newspaper by the time she was finished.

22
RAMONA

We placed the newly carved pumpkins on the porch, and I stepped back to admire our work. It was clear that I didn't carve all of them, but something in my chest swelled at the sight of our pumpkins butted up next to each other.

I indulged myself for the briefest of seconds, imagining what it would be like if the two of us always decorated the stoop every Halloween—*our* stoop, the one we owned together. What would it be like if this were just a normal night for us and not only a quick flash of stolen time?

"Not bad for a couple of townies." Iris's shoulder nudged mine, pulling me from my dangerously wistful daydream. "You need some candles floating around in the air. Really sets the tone."

"Using magic is against the rules," I chided.

"Didn't realize demons were rule-abiding citizens."

"If I cheated at every game, winning wouldn't be as much fun."

Her soft teasing tugged at an itch that was growing

more precarious the more comfortable she grew around me. It had been such a long time since I'd had someone, a long-term companion. Disregarding the friendships I held onto, it had been centuries since I had more than the occasional lover or one-night stand. Loneliness was par for the course as an immortal being. I'd outlived generations of humans, several vampires, and even some demons on this plane. But there was something special about the way Iris looked at me like I was an equal.

A hot equal, but an equal, nonetheless.

She didn't care that I was hellborn. And instead of feeling disrespected by her lack of adulation, I couldn't get enough of it.

"If there were no rules to follow, I wouldn't have a job," I finally said after a long pause.

"I guess I never thought about it like that."

"What do you think about?"

It was a wide-open question. She could say that she thought about her cat, that sassy little furball that clearly ran the apothecary with demanding authority. She could say she thought about Jordyn, or the coven, or the day-to-day of living in Maple Hollow.

She could say she thought about me.

She twisted her lips to one side and furrowed her brow, assessing the stoop again before saying, "I think I might have an idea if you have some paper, tape, and string?"

I didn't know what I was expecting, but that answer made me smile. "Come on. I'll let you raid my arts-and-crafts closet while I make you dinner."

"Dinner?"

"Yes? Don't witches eat?" I raised a brow at her. "Don't get any ideas, witchling. This doesn't count as the date you owe me. Our deal still stands. We're just on pause while I protect your life." Her cheeks flushed, and by Lucifer, that did things to me. "How does pasta sound?"

"Perfect."

I gave the street one more cursory glance, searching the shadows in case Esme was lurking within them. But when I couldn't sense the presence of any other beings, I led Iris back into the house. As we walked into the kitchen, I waved my hand and cleared the pumpkin guts from the island. Any normal human would have found the little trick awe-inspiring, but my little witchling didn't pay it any mind. She was right on my heels as I opened the small closet under the stairs to reveal a treasure trove of beads, fabric, yarn, and a myriad of other craft essentials.

"You really weren't kidding about having hobbies."

"Eternity can get tedious," I dryly replied. "Use whatever you like."

By the time I got the water boiling and took out the veggies to chop, Iris was already sitting down with an armful of supplies on the table. Our hands were busy with our individual tasks, and light conversation drifted between us while we cut and sautéed.

"Sorry if this sounds rude," Iris eventually said, piquing my interest, "but do demons have to eat and drink to survive?"

"No, but we enjoy the act just as much as any others we partake in." I shot her a suggestive look.

"Oh." Iris swept a lock of hair behind her ear, and I wondered how long I could elicit her blushing response. "So it's not boring?"

"Cooking is its own kind of magic, like any other potion

or intentional activity. It takes energy but also creates it. That's all magic is, after all."

"You make it sound so simple, but I've been learning how to use magic my entire life and will likely never master it."

"Do you want to master it? Is that a goal of yours?"

"I . . . I don't know. I was born to wield magic. What else would I do?"

"Is there anything else you always wished you could master instead of the art of magic? Like cooking or an instrument or a video game?"

Great. I'm asking about her life goals already. Soon, we'll be comparing star charts.

I wondered if anyone in her coven had ever given her a choice in the matter. There were plenty of witches who'd left the coven. Iris's little sister was dating the daughter of a witch who'd left, after all. Magic was certainly their primary calling, but I could tell that Iris had many talents that had nothing to do with the sparks that danced on her fingertips when she was angry or scared.

"You should explore more of your interests," I encouraged. But then I looked at the paper ghost she was hot gluing to a long string . . . and my Italian marble. "Though, I don't suggest art."

"Don't get smart with me," Iris jeered. "I may not have ultimate mastery of my own power yet, but I'm still deadly with a pair of scissors."

"Are you threatening to scissor me?"

Her gasp of surprise sent me into another fit of laughter.

"Ramona!" she chastised, waving the glue gun at me.

Lucifer, I loved the way her cheeks pinked up for me.

The timer on the oven took my attention away.

"Dinner's ready," I announced before I took a couple of plates out of the cupboard. "Wash your hands."

"Yes, ma'am." Iris slipped behind me, her hip brushing mine as she turned on the tap. The smell of her cut through the plump shrimp, lush butter, and wine sauce I was spooning over the nests of coiled spaghetti. She smelled like rosemary, amber, and incense—a warmth that mirrored her soul. Everything about her was inviting and cozy and tinged with electrifying spice.

"Wine?" I held up the bottle of the Chardonnay I'd used to make the sauce and Iris nodded.

There was over half the bottle left, and it would be a shame to waste it in the fridge. And I felt like I needed some liquid courage as I danced so close to something I was afraid to name.

I picked up the plates and set them on the island, where I ate all my meals. The table felt too formal and empty. Iris came to sit next to me and without hesitation began to dig into her shrimp scampi. She devoured half her plate before she slowed and gave a satisfactory hum.

I grinned, watching in delighted fascination as she feasted on my cooking.

"This is amazing, by the way," she complimented around through a mouthful. "I can't remember the last time someone cooked for me." She pushed at a shrimp on the edge of her plate.

"I can't remember the last time I cooked for someone." I stole a glance over at her and saw a twitch at the corner of her mouth.

"Did you ever cook for Esme?"

I had a feeling she wasn't talking just about cooking. "Never."

I could tell her line of questioning was far from over, so I offered an explanation that didn't feel like I was cutting my abdomen open and spilling my entrails all over my polished wood floor: "Esme and I became friends at a dark time in my existence. The Pope had just embraced the practice of exorcising demons and the like back to hell. It was relentless, not to mention painful. Nothing quite like being ripped out of a body. And every time I battled my way back earthside, having to start fresh, my ledgers wiped clean, I'd immediately be cornered by exorcists or hunters again. Very *en vogue* for the times. But then Esme saved me from an ambush in central Europe."

The memory of that night burned brightly. The blood flooding the alleyway, how she'd refused to drink from the men who'd called her an abomination. But spilling their blood and leaving it to rot had fed her in different ways too.

"It took us a few more run-ins to form a bond. I owed her my life and repaid her, then she repaid me. On and on, around the world we went until we ended up in New York City. By then, we were inseparable. But I was blinded by friendship and I didn't recognize that she was the reason hunters were always finding us. She left a trail of bodies in her wake. When we made our way to Maple Hollow, she'd promised to stop. To embrace a quieter life. She lied."

"That's when the hunter came to Maple Hollow," Iris supplied.

She was sitting so close to me now that our knees touched under the island. The barest contact had heat coursing through me.

I nodded. "The witches in the coven at the time helped banish her from the town, along with what was left of the vampire clan. She couldn't have returned unless someone powerful within several miles of the county line invited her back. I still have no idea who did it."

"Avery?" Iris mused. "She said she spotted her a few towns over. Maybe she did more than she's saying?"

"I don't think so."

"I'm surprised they trusted you enough to not invite her back."

I huffed out a bitter laugh. "Me too."

"Then who was it who welcomed her? Who's more powerful than you?"

"That is what I've been asking myself since the day of the knitting circle," I replied, the delicious meal souring in my stomach. "And I still don't have answers."

"We'll figure it out. Then I'll be out of your hair . . . and house."

I don't want that.

The knee-jerk reaction in my belly was proof.

I wanted her to stay.

I wanted her tucked away doing arts and crafts, laughing, and cooking until we crawled into our bed at the end of the night.

Together.

The simplest of simple pleasures, the most terrifying to attain.

But Iris wasn't here for that. No. She was only here for protection and a debt that she still owed . . . and perhaps the curiosity of what one night with a demon could be like.

23
IRIS

I offered to do the dishes after dinner. It was the least I could do after Ramona had made me one of the best meals of my life. She insisted that she load the dishwasher because she had a special agreement with the machine, and if I broke it, she'd make me her dish servant until it was fixed. Never mind that she could have it fixed with a wave of her hand or a call to the local repair ghoul. I suspected she enjoyed the ritual of it. I suspected even more that she'd have enjoyed keeping me chained to her kitchen sink for a week just for entertainment.

Having the lion's share of one and a half bottles of wine at dinner wasn't my smartest choice, but it was making me bold and rather warm all over.

Was demon wine stronger than normal wine? Surely, nothing was stronger than witch wine.

"So, where am I permitted to sleep now that I'm fed and thoroughly exhausted from arts and crafts?" I lazily dried my hands on a dish towel. "Your couch looks really fancy,

but with a few blankets, I'm sure I'll sleep just fine after I finish this." I held up the last two sips of wine in my glass and swigged it back.

"Do demons even have beds?" I mused. "Like, vampires have coffins and ghouls have graves. But you don't look like you'd enjoy getting dirty." My cheeks burned as soon as the words left my mouth, and I braced myself for her reply about just how dirty she could be.

I didn't miss the mischief that blazed in her side eye, but instead of rising to the bait, she said, "How about I take you on a tour of the house before we settle in and I kick your ass at checkers?"

I guffawed. "Are you actually an elderly woman possessing a demon?"

"I do go to bingo every once in a while." She shrugged. "But only if Mable is calling."

"Do zombies have some special bingo-calling abilities I'm not aware of?"

"Her cousin owns The Bloody Mary, so whoever wins gets a free round afterward."

"Ah."

With that, she walked out of the kitchen with a quick, "Come along," over her shoulder.

I hung the towel over the edge of the sink and caught up to her in the living room. Its modern styling reminded me of the waiting rooms in some corporate buildings. The angular couch and glass table were the main components of the austere room. There were a few pieces of art on the walls, but nothing as colorful as the floralginas in the kitchen.

"There is a bathroom just down the hall, across from the garage door. Nothing particularly notable unless you have a thing for Portuguese masonry," she announced and took a step toward the stairs. I had no idea what that meant. "There's also a linen closet that I suggest you stay away from unless you want to be transported to the fiery pits of the fifth circle of hell. It was an . . . impractical choice in hindsight, but nothing can be perfect."

Her sense of humor was so dry, I couldn't tell if she was joking or not.

And I didn't want to find out.

"Upstairs, there is another bathroom and two bedrooms, but there's only one room with a bed. Mine."

"Does the other room lead to the sixth circle of hell?"

Ramona only rolled her eyes. "No, but I do keep all my favorite . . . tools in there. So, for someone, it could be a special sort of hell."

The knots in my stomach twisted, from excitement or nerves, who knew, but I wasn't going in that room either. At least not tonight.

"There are towels under the sink," she said, a jarring return to a normal house tour after mentioning hell pits and torture rooms. "You can find a new toothbrush in the medicine cabinet. And fresh bed linens are in the closet there. No portals required."

I followed her to the top of the landing and peered over her shoulder. The space was lit by the large bay window at the end of the hall. Ramona opened the door to our right and stepped to the side for me. "This is the bathroom."

To no one's surprise, it looked straight out of a luxury hotel. The freestanding clawfoot bathtub could fit two people easily. I didn't want to think of how many people Ramona had managed to fit under the multiple shower-heads in the steam shower either.

"Could you . . . show me how it works?" I managed to breathe.

Her breath hit my ear as her luscious voice dropped lower. "Anything you want, my little witchling."

My.

The things that single word did to me.

Her hand brushed my hip as she walked past me, and the ember in my core blazed to life. The sound of water hitting the tile snapped me out of the fantasy of Ramona wet and dripping.

"Come closer so I can show you the action panel." She pointed to a small black rectangle on the wall, and even though it would have been better for my sanity to keep my distance, I obeyed. "These buttons control the temperature." She pressed the button twice, then took my hand to stick it under one of the streams of water. "Too cold?"

"Yes," was all I could muster as her damp fingertips caressed my wrist.

"Tell me when it's hot enough," she practically purred and pressed the button again.

"More," I said, something in my chest swelling and threatening to burst. She increased the heat again. "More." Her brow ticked up as if she were questioning my tolerance. "More." I was breathless and fighting the urge to pull us both into the shower. The word had become my mantra. It was all I wanted. "More."

Steam filled the small glass-enclosed space and floated out between us.

"Iris?"

I tilted my head to meet Ramona's gaze, but her eyes were fixed on my mouth. I hadn't realized how close she was, her lips a hair's breadth from my own and a question in her silver eyes.

Was that a question? The question? Or was it the final warning?

I didn't know and didn't care.

I couldn't take it anymore. All of this building and building inside of me was always going to lead us to this moment, teetering on the precipice of something neither of us could deny.

So instead of pulling away, I simply said the one word that had swarmed all my thoughts: "More."

Before I could close the distance, Ramona's body crashed into mine, pushing both of us into the shower.

Her kiss was vicious but passionate. Her soft lips demanded mine as a sacrifice.

I barely noticed the water drenching our clothes while our hands roamed. I couldn't decide which part of her to touch first, her hips, round ass, or the valley between her breasts that had always taunted me from the low necklines of her shirts. The madness in me was like nothing I'd ever felt before. I wanted to memorize every inch of her.

I eagerly pulled at the hem of my shirt, and that was the catalyst that turned our frenzy into an inferno.

Ramona let out a needy little growl and I knew her thoughts matched my own: *No more messing around. I need you.*

The buttons of her shirt popped, fabric tore, and pants and underwear magically slid down our bodies and dropped to a sopping pile at our feet.

Thank fuck for magic.

With a possessive grip, Ramona took hold of my wet hair and deepened our kiss, bringing our naked bodies together.

Her knee wedged between mine, and her hand slipped between my legs.

Slick fingers circled my clit, making me moan into her mouth. Goddess, I was already right on the edge of an orgasm. She barely needed to touch me after edging me all day. But her fingers worked me as if she knew exactly what I needed.

The mounting pressure in my belly tipped as she pushed her fingers inside of me and commanded, "Come undone for me."

Stars burst. Planets collided. And the world-rearranging orgasm had her taking all of my weight, pinning me to the wall when my knees gave out.

The rush was like nothing I'd ever felt. Wave after wave of pleasure.

If I didn't already know magic was real, I would now.

Ramona's kisses turned soft and tender before she pulled away and let me bask in the afterglow of the best orgasm of my life. But when I finally managed to open my eyes and steady my legs, I was rewarded with a full view of Ramona's gloriously naked body. She was lithe and soft and curved in all the right ways—a body perfectly molded to fit against mine.

As if reading my thoughts, the demon smiled wickedly and reached over my head to retrieve an expensive-looking bottle of body wash. She squirted a bit into her palm before handing it to me and lathering the soap. It smelled like her: musky, floral, and a little bit of spice. When her palms were full of bubbles, she rubbed my shoulders and then moved down to my chest, breasts, and belly. All the while, our eyes never left each other's.

The feeling of her hands massaging the soapy lather across my skin was its own sort of ecstasy.

When she deemed me sufficiently covered, she pulled me under the water, taking her time to rinse away the soap before turning off the shower and returning the bottle to the shelf. She stepped out first, grabbed two towels from under the sink, then wrapped one around me then one around herself.

We didn't need words. I was still glowy from what had just happened, although I was a bit disappointed that we were covered up again. I was far from ready for this night to be over.

But then she took my hand and led me out of the bathroom and through a door across the hall. As soon as the light came on, I realized it was her bedroom. My hair was dripping and I worried I would somehow ruin her bedding, but any protest I had disappeared when Ramona pulled open a drawer next to her bed and pulled out not one, not two, but three straps: one a cognac leather, one a studded bloodred, and one an opalescent silver that matched her eyes.

She smirked. "Pick your poison, witch."

She slid open the drawer below and I was greeted with an array of dildos in varying shapes and sizes.

My mouth watered.

Now this is a choose-your-own adventure I could get behind.

The purple one was small and thin but deliciously curved. The next was thick, long, and ribbed. And like some sort of porno version of *Goldilocks and the Three Bears*, the third looked just right. The tentacle-looking attachment had suction cups on the underside, an undulating bulge in the middle, and a small twist at the end to hit all the right spots.

I picked up the dildo and gave it a testing squeeze as my core clenched. "This one?"

"Good choice," Ramona said approvingly. "It vibrates."

With a snap of her fingers, the opalescent harness was wrapped around her waist, and the toy vanished from my fingers only to reappear perfectly positioned in the ring between her legs. The harness fit her like a glove, and she didn't have to split her attention between sustaining the mood while fiddling with the buckles and trying to play it off like she'd *meant* to step into the wrong leg hole.

All bless the goddess of lesbian magic.

Ramona pulled at my towel with desperation, the two of us stumbling backward toward the bed. When the backs of my thighs hit the mattress, her hand shot out to catch the nape of my neck and lower me onto the soft satin sheets.

Hell had nothing on the heat in her eyes when she looked at me.

"Open your legs for me," she ordered, and I did as she commanded, my heart fluttering in my chest. "Good girl."

She notched the tip of the tentacle at my entrance and pulsed. The vibrations buzzed across my sensitive flesh, and my hips rose to meet hers, but she pulled back, taunting. She climbed farther onto the bed, hovering over me as she kissed a line down my jaw and throat to my chest and sucked a nipple into her mouth.

I bit down on my lip to quell the curse clawing up my throat. Her tongue flicked and her teeth nipped until I was close to coming just from those sensations alone.

"Ramona," I moaned. "Please."

She let out a triumphant groan before she thrust her hips and the tentacle filled me.

"Oh fuck!" I was pulled down by the undertow of sensations, already knowing that the best orgasm of my life was about to be topped.

Those vibrating suckers hit *all* the right nerves.

Ramona's breath was ragged, a satisfied hum on her lips as she pumped in and out until I was on the brink of another blinding orgasm. When the wave of pleasure took hold, I cried out, my voice echoing off the walls. I didn't know how long I made those euphoric sounds, but by the time Ramona slowed her thrusts, my throat was hoarse, my body boneless and sated.

The haze started to fade, and our mouths met again as my body went slack. Ramona eased the toy out of me and over my still-sensitive nerves, causing me to shiver. A quick moment later, her warmth returned as she rolled to her side and gathered me against her.

"Wow," was all I could manage.

She huffed a laugh. "Yeah?"

The wine and euphoria felt thick in my blood but loosened my lips. "I waited a whole year when we could've been doing that the whole time?"

She laughed and pulled me closer. "We'll have to make up for lost time, then, I guess."

"Right now?" I teased even as I stifled a yawn.

"I think you should get some sleep first." She kissed my temple, the action surprisingly tender. "Let me tuck you in, red."

"You're not just going to leave me alone in here, right?" I wasn't ready for her to exit our little lust-filled bubble. I knew the moment she left this room, reality would set in, and I would abandon sleep to overthink every moment of this evening and what it meant . . . and worse, what it didn't mean.

Ramona nuzzled my hair, sleepily resting her cheek atop my head. "Not a chance, love."

Those four words blanketed my looming anxiety, tucking it away, safe and sound, for some other time.

Together, we settled under the blankets and entwined our legs and arms. She pulled me into her chest, and I fell fast asleep to the sound of her heart, the perfect tempo to plunge me into dreams of a world where we did this every night.

24
IRIS

There was no better sleep aid than being wrapped in the arms of a gorgeous woman. I had no idea how long I'd slept. The sky that peeked between the sleek grey curtains flirted with dawn. I didn't want to get up—ever. Once this night between us ended, would we ever get another? Maybe I could go full cliche sapphic date and roll this morning into a brunch, into window shopping, into an early dinner, into another wild, fun night, and then, after a five-day-long date, we just kind of lived together? It had happened to me before ...

But Ramona wasn't a lovesick witch or nymph or werewolf or any of the other paranormals I'd dated before. I felt it in my bones: this was different. And I was already preemptively heartbroken about it ending.

But even with all of that angst rolling around my brain, my bladder won out and I decided to get up. I disentangled myself from Ramona's sleepy limbs and laughed when she clung to me for a second like she didn't want me to go.

I kissed her shoulder, and one of her cheeks dimpled.

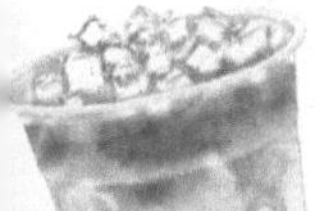

"I'm just going to get some water." *And to piss like a racehorse, but she didn't need to know. Quiet luxury and all that.* "Go back to sleep."

"I'm a demon," she countered in a grumpy, raspy voice, her eyes still closed. "I don't need to sleep."

Still, I slunk to the tobacco leather wingback in the corner and grabbed the navy-blue sweater hanging over the arm.

"Can I wear this?" I whispered into the dark room, holding up the chunky knit.

Ramona sat up against the headboard and slicked her mussed hair off her face. "I'd prefer you wear nothing at all," she purred, folding her arms. "But if you must, you might as well wear that one." I was already tugging the sweater over my head when she added, "I made it for you, after all."

I froze as the hemline dropped to midthigh. "You made this for me?" I studied the soft sweater, the moon phases embroidered in silver across the chest. *The same silver as Ramona's eyes.*

"I must confess I had fantasies of you wearing nothing but my sweater,"—Ramona drank me in, indulging herself in every inch of exposed skin—"but they didn't do you justice."

"This is so beautiful. I—" Emotions constricted in my throat, choking out the words. I looked at her and my eyes hooked as I prowled back toward her.

She arched a brow. "I thought you wanted to get a drink of water?"

"After," I said.

"After what?"

"After you fuck me in the sweater you made for me," I crooned, crawling up the bed toward her.

Mischievous delight filled her eyes as she grabbed me by the waist and pulled me down on the bed. We let our hands and mouths explore until sweat coated our skin. She tasted like temptation and the sweetest of sins. Hearing her shout my name as her body shuddered around my fingers was enough for me to accept any damnation that she'd brought me.

The sun was peeking through the curtains by the time I managed to get up for that glass of water—and finally empty my bladder, which was probably a good idea after what we'd just done. The vivid echoes of Ramona midorgasm flashed through my mind, and I couldn't help but beam with a strange sort of pride that I could make her come undone just as much as she did me.

A sated smile affixed to my lips, I practically floated down the stairs toward the kitchen.

It hadn't even been twelve hours, but I already felt familiar with her home. The artistic minimalism made it easy to navigate the space. Part of me hoped Esme would take her sweet time haunting Maple Hollow if it meant I was "forced" to be stuck in this place a little while longer.

I found a glass in her very neatly arranged cupboard, and as I filled the water, I heard the telltale click of Ramona's designer shoes approaching. A little flare of disappointment bloomed in my belly that she'd already gotten dressed.

Oh well. All the more fun to peel off her clothes again.

"Did you come down here to make me breakfast? Because I'm starving," I said with a laugh as I turned off the tap. "I'm going to need to refuel after last night."

But when I turned around, it wasn't Ramona standing there at all.

25
RAMONA

At the sound of Iris's scream, I bolted into the kitchen in nothing but a bra and briefs. Panic lanced through me when I heard glass shatter. Was she hurt? Did she faint? Did a portal to hell secretly open in my linen closet?

Those were the only three things I could guess as I ran, but what I saw when I entered the kitchen made my heart plummet.

"No."

Iris was held by the throat, her back pinned to her captor's chest—a captor who was the only other person who could get into my house.

Terror morphed into confusion. What in the fuck?

"Naphula," I growled. "Let. Her. Go."

My best friend squeezed the witch's throat tighter in response. Iris's eyes bulged in panic, the vein in her forehead pulsing.

"Naphula. Listen to me." I tried speaking like I was

calming a skittish horse, but I was beginning to suspect my friend's mind wasn't in the building with us.

Naphula's glassy eyes were unfocused and stared blankly at . . . nothing. They were empty voids that held no hellfire, just blank spaces that reflected the morning light like obsidian mirrors. It was as if her body were just the shell of my best friend, a conduit, a vessel for another. I didn't know if she had chosen to work for Esme or whether she was under the vampire's curse, but in that moment, with her hand around Iris's throat, I didn't care.

"Naphula, let her go!" I shouted this time, but she didn't move. My mind reeled with all my potential plans of action, but each one ended with Naphula snapping Iris's neck. "If you try to take her, I will slit your throat right here and now. Do you hear me? Damn our friendship to hell."

"Ramona—" Iris rasped as Naphula's grip constricted, threatening to choke the life out of her.

The air around them started whirring, and my gut plummeted.

"No, no, no!" I yelled, rushing to grab Iris, but I couldn't reach her in time.

She and Naphula vanished before my eyes, leaving no traceable essence for me to follow.

Gone.

"Fuck!" I picked up a vase of roses from the island and slammed it into the wall. The spray of water and ceramic shards joined the shattered glass where Iris had dropped her drink.

How could I have let this happen?

I bolted up the stairs to my room and threw on the first items of clothing I could find. Then I shoved my feet into my running shoes and tied them with a wave of my shaking hand before I took the steps two at a time to my front door.

My rage burned brighter than the forges of hell. I would turn the entire town upside down to find them.

Goose bumps rose on my arms as I ran toward the center of town, a wave of nausea curdling my stomach. It was eerily calm, even for this early in the morning.

Too empty. Too calm.

All the while, a vein of evil was running in the undercurrent of our sleepy town.

Esme and Naphula had taken Iris somewhere, and even if I had to call in every soul and every favor I'd ever collected to find them, so help me Lucifer, I would.

My lungs burned, but I pushed harder until I practically crashed into Agnes just outside the antique shop.

"Ramona?" she asked, instantly concerned. "What's going on?"

"Naphula took Iris," I huffed, cursing my human form and the fact that I couldn't use portal magic the same way Naphula could. She was the perfect tool for Esme—my friend and confidante, a demon with incredible magic, the keeper of all of my secrets . . .

"Naphula?" Agnes balked. "But I thought it was Esme we were looking for—"

"She'd been cursed," I gritted out before breaking into a sprint. "Her eyes, there was nothing behind them. She wasn't herself. It was as if she couldn't even hear me."

"A mind-control curse," Agnes said with an affirming nod. The elderly vampire was able to keep a preternatural pace with me without even trying. "Must be. I'll tell the others. We'll find them." She broke off at the town square with military precision as I kept running. "Billy!" I heard her yell. "Get the phone tree, we've got a missing witch!"

Even through my panic, I knew half of Maple Hollow would be awake and on the hunt for Iris within the hour. Hopefully, the wolves could track her scent, or the witches could perform a location spell on her, but I kept running.

Because I had to. I couldn't just wait, helpless, hoping that she would be alright.

Esme didn't have Naphula break Iris's sigil like the others. They'd taken Iris from me because Esme wanted to use Iris to hurt me. And after that—

No, I couldn't think about what would happen to Iris. I couldn't think about her being taken away from me— permanently. Not after everything felt right for the first time in longer than I could remember.

So I just kept running. Because I needed Iris. Because I loved her.

I let out a feral growl at that.

I loved her.

The thought made my brain split in two.

I didn't think love was an emotion I was capable of; I didn't think it would ever exist in me. Sex, sure. Desire, most definitely. But love? No.

But this feeling—like my heart was exploding through my ribs, like my mind was always reaching for her, even when she was in my arms, like I wanted to fuse my soul with hers and even that wouldn't be enough—was *love*, wasn't it?

Seven Hells, I thought love would feel a lot less like torture, but maybe the two were one and the same.

Nothing would be right again until Iris was safe in my arms.

It was nonsensical. Iris was fun and lighthearted, brave

and silly, smart and joyful and all kinds of sunshine-y chaos, and I was none of those things. But she made me want to be. She made me excited about every possibility. For her, I wanted to be *everything*.

I halted abruptly. A thought had me skidding into the middle of the dewy square, and then I was turning toward the pumpkin patch and picking up speed.

Esme needed a remote location within the town limits to hide out, and Randy had said he was pretty sure someone was squatting at the house in the patch.

Maybe they weren't ghouls after all . . .

26
IRIS

All I could see was Ramona's furious, terrified face as the world went black. I thought I knew what her anger looked like, but it was nothing compared to the ferocity that had radiated from her like heat waves in a desert. She'd looked as if she were going to tear the other demon to shreds, reconstitute her, then shred her apart all over again. *For me.* Whatever fear had flashed through me at being taken was superseded by that thought: *the most fero-cious demon in hell and on Earth was coming to get me.*

When I came to, my head was throbbing and my stomach was sloshing like a burbling washing machine. Jumping through time and space was not meant for human —or witch—bodies. I felt like I'd just run a marathon, my corporeal vessel put through the wringer. I groaned, my throat hoarse, and I wondered how long I'd been out. The soft glow of sunlight that peeked through the slats of the building was my only clue. Judging by the sharp angle, I surmised it was just after dawn. It was only when I

attempted to lift my aching head that I realized my hands were tied to a hook on the wall above me.

What the . . .

I yanked on my itchy rope bindings, testing them. I still wore nothing but Ramona's blue sweater, which barely covered my ass as I gathered my legs under me. I took in the room as my head cleared. I surveyed the dirt floor, slats of splintering wood, the ladder that stretched up to a loft with an unmade bed . . . and bucketfuls of rusty pumpkin carving tools.

It all came flooding back to me.

"Naphula." I searched for her as my depth perception started to recover. "What the fuck have you done?"

My bleary eyes finally landed on the demon standing in the corner, her eyes glazed and completely black. She looked like a vacant zombie . . . although that wasn't really fair to our local zombie bartender.

I'd seen that look before. Had learned all about it at the summer camp for witches. That was how I knew for certain that Naphula was under some sort of curse.

"So that's how she's doing it," I murmured, realization lighting up my senses. "Using a demon to do her dirty work. Clever, Esme. She must've known Ramona wouldn't have warded her house against her best friend."

Naphula didn't react at all to my voice. She just waited like a robot for her next command.

Shit. That was some seriously dark magic if even a demon couldn't fight it.

I wondered how long she'd been under Esme's curse, how atrophied her ability to fight back had become. There was a reason this kind of magic had been forbidden by local coven bylaws. It wouldn't only potentially kill Naphula if she was kept under its grip for much longer, but Esme could just as soon destroy herself with this curse as much as wield it.

"Esme," I croaked as loud as I could, trying to summon the vampire. But the air remained still—as did my silent demonic babysitter, who didn't so much as flinch.

I gritted my teeth. This bitch. She'd come back into town, upended Ramona's life—and by extension, my own—and now she thought could just kill me?

Not happening. You've messed with the wrong witch.

Fuming, I gathered the magical energy within me and concentrated it in my fingertips. Small sparks sizzled above my head. My magic felt both relieved and eager to be unleashed.

"*Dolor*," I called in Latin. "*Afferte mihi sanguinem.*"

Naphula twitched as if bitten by a mosquito. It was the smallest warning, but the dark ooze of demon blood appeared as a small nick on her cheek.

"Aha!" I exclaimed with a knowing nod. "Gotcha, bitch."

I started chanting louder, striking another blow and splitting Naphula's lip. I knew the demon could take it, probably was grateful I was doing it, even as I beat her to a bloody pulp. The threat to the vessel would bring her consciousness to the surface and pull her out of Esme's control. I hoped it royally pissed off the vampire as she felt her influence slipping away with the same pain I was inflicting.

"Stop," Naphula growled, her voice and face contorting, distorted by the curse. "I said stop, you fucking witch."

I let out my patented witch cackle, glee igniting my magic.

"You didn't bring me here to fuck around, Esme," I crowed. "Fight me."

Naphula lurched forward, her movements sharp and erratic, as if two puppeteers were battling for control of her strings. I pushed harder, spurred on by the knowledge that the connection between her and Esme was fracturing. With a snap of my fingers, I released my useless bindings. The fools had tied me up like I was a human. A simple rope would never stop a witch. They would have needed more than that to keep me held down.

I rose to my feet just as Naphula got within arm's reach of me. I cocked my fist and swung, hitting her with a hard uppercut to the jaw that had her stumbling backward and my knuckles shooting with a satisfying flash of pain. I steadied myself on my feet, fire magic swirling around my hands.

Naphula shook her head, bits of white and silver bleeding through the black veil in her eyes before disappearing again.

"Fight it, Naphula," I commanded. Then I spoke to Esme again, a wicked smile pulling my lips. "Come on, bloodsucker," I snarled. "Let's play."

27
RAMONA

I tore across the pumpkin patch, kicking up leaves in my wake. I'd never raced this fast in my life.

Please, please, please. Let her be safe.

My lungs burned as I silently begged and bargained while I ran.

Whatever needs to happen, whatever I need to do. Please, to every devil in every circle of hell, let this hunch be right.

As I approached the building, I saw no signs of movement, heard no calls of distress.

Fear choked me in its viselike grip.

I ate up the distance to the rickety door and threw it open, then ran inside. My cursed meat suit was flooded with endorphins and ready to take on Naphula, Esme, and any other creature standing in the way of my girl. But when I got there, I spotted Iris, wearing nothing but the sweater I'd knitted for her, leaning against the central beam with her arms crossed while she stared smugly at bloodied and tied-up Naphula.

"Oh, hey," Iris said like we'd bumped into each other at the library.

"Hey?"

She'd been kidnapped from my house. This was the most terrifying moment of my immortal life. And all she said was *hey*?

"I told you, demon." Iris shrugged. "I'm a powerful witch. I can take care of myself."

All the panic ebbed and melted to something like lust-addled relief as I crossed the distance to that *powerful witch*. Locking her in my sights, I grabbed Iris by the back of the neck and pinned her to the beam behind her. My tongue delved into her mouth, and I kissed her with all the relief and desperation that had been churning within me.

They'd taken her. They'd taken her *from me*, and the fear of losing her had made all of my inexplicable feelings crystal clear.

She was here, safe, strong, and as wicked as I was in every way. And I loved her. Simple as that.

I finally pulled away enough to murmur against her lips, "I want to fuck you so badly right now, but we need to deal with this whole vampire thing first."

Iris's hands slid up my sides as if she couldn't stop herself from touching me—*torturing me*—but with a disgruntled sigh, she dropped them. "Later?"

"Later," I promised. "And many times after that, witchling."

I took a step back, needing to put some distance between us before my hands delved under the hem of her sweater and slid up her—

Naphula groaned from behind us.

I turned to see her gasp, her eyes returning to their normal color.

"Ramona. I—I'm sorry," Naphula spluttered. "I didn't mean—I didn't know what I was doing—"

Blood trailed from her nose and several cuts on her face. I wasn't sure if they were inflicted by Esme or Iris.

"What happened?" I asked, walking over to her.

"No, don't," Naphula warned, terror in her voice. She wiggled against her binds, but the rope was illuminated with a familiar glow that I knew was Iris's magic keeping them in place. "I can't fight her. I don't know when the trance will take hold again. You need to keep me tied up until you break the curse she's using to contain me."

"Esme." I balled my hands into fists. "She's not content with stealing my marks and hurting my girlfriend. She needs to go after my best friend too."

"Did you just call me your girlfriend?" Iris piped up from behind me.

It was my turn for a furious blush to burn across my face. "Well, I—"

"I like it," Iris offered before I had time to spiral out about my feelings being unrequited.

She liked it. She liked the thought of being mine.

"Can you two lovebirds break this damned curse on me before you fuck each other? Please?" Naphula snapped. "Also—" She stretched her head to look around me and glare at Iris. "If you break my best friend's heart, I will kill you."

"You've already tried to kill me," Iris pointed out with a shit-eating grin. *That's my girl.* "And look how that turned out for you." Damn, she was really not helping quell my libido with that sexy retort, especially when her green eyes flitted to mine. "But I have no intention of breaking any hearts."

At those words, an overwhelming flood of emotions rushed over me. It felt so sudden yet inevitable at the same time.

I leaned in—

"Ramona!" Naphula cut in. "Where's a fucking ice bucket when I need it, goddammit? Like, I'm happy for you, but seriously, get your shit together. I don't know how much time we have before I go full-on *Manchurian Candidate* again."

"Okay, okay," I grumbled, frustrated that I couldn't indulge in this moment.

I wanted to tell Iris that I had no intention of breaking her heart either.

I wanted to share with her the million secret, scary things that she gave me the confidence to finally say aloud.

But breaking vampiric curses came first. That was the sensible thing to do.

I turned fully to put Iris out of my view, then said to Naphula, "Start at the beginning. How did Esme even get close enough to you to place a curse on you in the first place?"

"I was summoned to make a deal. The mark was cloaked, not that unusual in our line of work." She was right; it was common for powerful beings to shield their identities, but it was still dangerous. I'd scold her about that later. "The mark wanted me to help her get revenge on someone, but because she's a vampire, she had no soul to give."

"What could possibly be as valuable as a soul?" Iris asked.

My pulse quickened. "She gave you a promise. An exchange. Favor for favor?"

"Yes," Naphula admitted, hanging her head. "She said she could help me block out any remaining, uh, feelings I had for . . . someone."

"Naphula, no." I groaned, rubbing my eyes in frustration. "You opened up your mind to a cloaked vampire for that? Why didn't you just come to me instead?"

A sheepish expression crossed my friend's face. "The circumstances were too embarrassing to tell you about. Not again."

"This is about Eloise?" I said, exasperated. "You'd rather wipe your crush from your memory than be honest with her?"

"See? This is why I didn't tell you!" Naphula snapped back. "You don't understand what it's like to be in the thrall of a lesbian werewolf, okay? Also, talk about hypocritical, accusing me of being afraid to admit my feelings."

Shame chased away my anger. She was right. Worse, I'd failed my friend when she'd needed me the most, and my sanctimonious judgment had left the perfect opening for Esme to attack.

Remorse softened my tone. "I'm sorry I ever let you doubt that we could've figured it out. Together."

"I was desperate, Mona." She shook her head as she looked between Iris and me. "I *know* you know what it feels like when someone hijacks your emotions like that. I thought it was the out I needed."

"Well, you having to deal with Wyatt will be punishment enough," I reminded her. "Especially if he finds out that the reason for breaking my sigil was because of your feelings for his sister."

"Agnes is going to feed off this gossip for *months*," Iris muttered.

"I didn't know I was going to be forced to attack anyone!" Naphula barked. "I tried to resist Esme, but the curse was too strong. The second I shook her hand, I welcomed her into my mind, and she did more than just erase the feelings." Her throat bobbed. "I lost so much time. At first, I thought it was a few too many drinks, but then things weren't stacking up. I'd wake up in bed with dirt beneath my fingernails, blood in my hair . . . I have no idea what she made me do."

"How long has this been going on?"

"Two months."

"Two *months*?" I howled. "Why didn't you tell me?"

"Because after I realized who she was, I couldn't. I couldn't bear the thought that you'd see me as weak."

"I'm supposed to be your best friend," I countered. "I'm the person that helps you bury the bodies, Naph. No matter what you're going through. Friends kill our enemies together, always."

"That is both very sweet and very upsetting," Iris murmured.

"And the feelings for Eloise are really gone?" My question brought her attention back to me.

"They were. Until I saw her again. When we—"

"You're fucking the baker!" Iris whisper-squealed. "Jordyn's gonna die when I tell her."

"I'm sorry, Mona." Naphula ignored my elated witch. "I knew I should've never agreed, and by the time I summoned the courage to tell you, Esme had caught on and her magic wouldn't let me get the words out."

I looked down at Iris. "Can you break this curse?"

"Not alone." She jutted her chin at all the bruises and cuts on Naphula's face and jaw. "We need to gather the whole coven to have any chance. This is very dark magic. It would be faster to kill Esme."

"I like that idea better. Quick and dirty," I said with a wink.

"You better stop winking at me," she warned, and I could see flashbacks of the night before strobing behind her eyes.

"Maybe just kill me," Naphula grumbled. "I can't take this anymore."

"Alright, alright." I snorted. "Is there a way to bring Esme here?"

"There is," Naphula replied. "I can contact her through my mind, tell her that I've got Iris, and we can rendezvous to deliver her."

"I'm not using her as bait."

"Oh, come on," Iris countered. "Look at me! I make great bait. I lured you here and I barely had to try."

"You didn't *lure* me here. You were taken from my house and I had to come find you."

"The witch waited for you to come find us." Naphula bit back a grin. "We were sitting here for at least twenty minutes before you showed up."

I pinched the bridge of my nose. The last thing I needed was these two in cahoots.

"Fine. Agree to a drop-off point and we'll ambush Esme there." I turned back to Iris and pointed at her. "You can be the bait if you put some pants on first."

She saluted me. "Yes, ma'am."

"Lucifer, help me. What have I gotten myself into with you, little witch?"

28

IRIS

I knelt between the graves, hands tied behind my back. I was wearing a pair of leggings that Ramona had pulled from some void realm for me. I was still barefoot though. Apparently, shoes weren't in her pocket realm's purview. But I couldn't even feel the autumnal chill with the rush of adrenaline that pulsed through me with each sound of crunching leaves that hit my ears.

The rogue vampire would arrive any minute now.

Naphula stood over me, working her jaw as she scanned the misty graveyard.

Finally, a voice cut through the eerie silence. "You caught the little bitch," a lilting feminine voice called. "Good. I was worried for a second there that you couldn't handle it, demon."

Naphula glared in the direction of the voice. "After this, we're done, Esme. I've made good on my end of the deal."

Esme's sharp cackle echoed through the early dawn. "You still think it's a deal that binds you to me? You demons are so simple." She tsked. "No, no. I *own* you now, Naphula."

Naphula stiffened. "I agreed to let you erase certain . . . things from my mind in exchange for four favors. I've broken three sigils for you and collected the witch. Four. The deal has ended."

"I love the way you demons think in such black and white," Esme mused. "Your wording is so careful, your deals so precise. But my magic is messy. I didn't just make a deal with you, simple demon. We aren't playing on your turf. I *cursed* you. You opened the door of your mind to me and I walked through." A wicked laugh cut through the night air. "Your mind is mine forever."

With that menacing omission, her figure emerged from the mist. Pale skin, flowing brunette waves, a black turtleneck, and a navy peacoat. Esme was an odd mishmash of styles, as if having collected them over many centuries.

Her eyes landed on me and held. "So you're the thing that's keeping her here." She cocked her head as she considered me. "I thought she'd be more formidable, Ramona," Esme called louder, turning in a circle. "Oh, come on, I know you're here somewhere. Don't be shy. Show your face."

"Enough of this, Esme." Ramona darted out from behind a gnarled elm tree. "Let them go. Both of them."

"Are you going to come with me?"

"No."

Esme pursed her lips. "I'm disappointed in you, Ramona. You used to be fearsome."

Ramona balled her fists. "Let me show you how fearsome I am still."

"We could rule this town and a dozen others like it, old friend. Why can't you see how powerful we could be?" She shook her head. "I don't want to do this without you." Her eyes darkened. "But I will if I have to."

"I know you will never understand this, Esme," Ramona said. "But this constant quest for more will always leave you hungry." Her eyes flitted to me for the barest second, as if she couldn't help herself. "I've found true happiness here. I've found meaning. And I won't sacrifice it for any quest for power or hollow bloodlust."

"Your happiness is fleeting, Ramona." Esme let out an incredulous laugh. "You've tied your meaning to a mortal."

"And I do it gladly," Ramona shouted as my breath became frantic at her declaration. "Every second her heart beats is beautiful, and I want to be a part of all she is willing to give to me."

"*Every second her heart beats* . . . Fine then. Have it your way." Esme flashed her teeth as she looked at me and snapped her fingers. "Naphula, kill her."

My heart lurched into my throat as I ducked just in time to miss the blow from the demon. I didn't even have a moment to process Ramona's words as I somersaulted forward. The command seemed to take Naphula and I both by surprise. What a terrible moment to assume Esme's grasp on the demon's mind had ended along with their deal.

I brought my bound hands to the front and leaped to my feet. Bringing all my magic to the fore, I blocked each of Naphula's attacks, but she wasn't dissuaded. The proximity to her puppet master must've made the commands that much harder to disobey. Each of my surges of magic ricocheted off Naphula and she still kept charging.

Meanwhile, Esme had taken the distraction as the perfect time to pounce. In half a second, Esme had Ramona flat on her back. The vampire moved with breathtaking speed, faster even than most of the supernatural creatures that dwelled in the town.

"You always were a loner, Esme," Ramona said, unbothered by the hand squeezing her throat. "You can't bear that I've found belonging. I know why you're really here. Your coven kicked you out, didn't they?"

"They were growing soft," Esme seethed. "I need someone stronger. You can be my coven now."

"Your selfishness is what's going to get you killed," Ramona rasped, gripping the wrist of the hand that choked her.

Esme threw her head back and laughed. The madness in her voice sent a surge of energy into Naphula, who snatched my ankle, toppling me to the ground.

Esme gripped Ramona's chin, forcing her to look over at us. "Watch your so-called best friend kill your little witch, then herself. A grand finale to your last attachments, Ramona. Then you'll finally be free."

Naphula pulled me underneath her frame, shoving me into the soft dirt of a fresh grave while I shrieked.

"You forget one thing, Esme," Ramona gritted out. "I don't just have two friends. I have this whole fucking town. Now!"

At her signal, the resident of Maple Hollow shot up from behind the graves. An army of supernatural residents spread out, dotting the rolling hills of gravestones far in the distance.

"What the—" Esme's words were drowned out by a mishmash of odd and zany war cries as the townspeople held up everything from pitchforks to rolling pins and began running to our aid.

"This town is a family," Ramona snarled. She bucked off a distracted Esme and shot to her feet. "And we don't let anyone mess with our family."

Cheers—and a few howls—rang throughout the grave-yard. Everyone hidden in the distant halo, ringing the open space, closed in. They'd kept their distance so as not to alert the rogue vampire of their presence, but I suspected she'd been so arrogant and single-minded, she hadn't even been looking for those lurking in the periphery.

With Esme's mind distracted, Naphula was finally susceptible to my magic. I sent a blast directly to her chest and scrambled to my feet, making a beeline toward Ramona. Naphula swiped the back of my sweater, but I evaded her and ran as fast as my legs could take me.

"Wyatt!" I called, and the werewolf leaped out from behind an elm tree, followed by three pack members holding nets and rope. "Get her, boys!" I bolted past them as they rushed Naphula, the werewolves easily restraining her in her stupefied state.

I kept running until I reached Ramona's side, and then she looped her arm around my waist as she smiled at her cornered foe. Esme's face fell as she whirled, turning in each direction only to find witches, monsters, and werewolves creeping closer and closer.

Agnes emerged at the head of the vampire coven. "We banished you from this town, Esme, for what your callous recklessness brought upon our kind and all other monsters who found safety here."

"Just let Ramona and me go, and I promise I will never return," Esme pleaded, holding up her hands in surrender.

"Ramona belongs with us. Here." Agnes's eyes darkened. "We claim her as her true family."

Ramona's hand on my side instinctively squeezed. It was such a subtle action, but I knew how badly she needed to hear those words and the hoots of agreement from the rest of the town.

"But banishment is clearly not enough, Esme." Agnes advanced and lifted a sharpened stake. "For the destruction you've wrought on your unwelcome return, for breaking the codes set forth by the covens both witch and vampire, and for ignoring the warnings therein, we condemn you to death."

Esme's wide eyes frantically searched the crowd before they landed on an opening in the circle we'd formed around her, and she bolted toward the haunted woods.

"Shit!" I cursed as the vampire sprinted across the graveyard with preternatural speed. "Randy!"

"On it!" A bellow and galloping hooves sounded before Randy appeared astride his horse. They raced behind Esme as Randy lifted his glowing head in his hand.

"He's not going to—" Ramona started.

"Of course he is," I answered.

Randy lobbed his pumpkin head at Esme, and when it collided with the back of her skull, the force of it sent her sprawling into a headstone.

Jordyn and Harlow dashed toward her from a nearby grave.

"Broom!" Jordyn screeched, and then her broomstick was whizzing through the air and into Jordyn's waiting hand. Immediately, she snapped it over her knee and drove the splintered end into Esme's back.

With a wail, the vampire disintegrated into nothing but ash.

"Holy shit," Harlow said, staring wide-eyed at the ground. "Did you just Buffy a freaking vampire?"

Jordyn dusted herself off before turning toward her girlfriend with a smug smile. Witchly pride bloomed in my chest.

Naphula collapsed to the ground, holding her head in her hands and I instinctively dove to her side, hands hovering over her to search for injury. Her body was whole, but her mind fractured. Naphula sat up with a groan, dropping her head in her hands like she was nursing the worst hangover of her life.

"Is she okay?" Ramona asked, breathlessly reaching my side and pulling me into a tight hug. There was such desperation in her hold, as if her very arms needed proof that I was alright.

I pulled her closer and buried my face in the crook of her neck, murmuring, "Nothing an apothecary witch can't mend."

"Impressive," Ramona said, brushing a kiss to my temple.

"I told you. Don't mess with witches."

"I'm sorry I ever doubted you." She pulled back to search my eyes. Her brows were pinched together, and there was something in her stormy expression that I couldn't name . . . or maybe I was too afraid that I knew exactly what it was and that I felt it just as fiercely in return. "I . . ." Her eyes fell to my lips, like she was warring with herself. ". . . need to go thank everyone."

I cleared my throat, stepping out of her embrace. "Yeah, good idea."

Sadness and relief mixed on her face as she turned and walked toward the group of celebrating townsfolk. Their cheers and excitement filled the graveyard.

Jordyn appeared by my side. "You're looking none the worse for wear. Are you okay? Are you hurt?"

I gave her a weak smile. "A few scrapes but nothing serious." I didn't bother trying to hide the cauldron of mixed feelings bubbling inside of me.

She wrapped an arm around my shoulder and brought me in for a squeeze. "Nothing a hot cup of tea and a good sleep can't fix, huh?"

I was exhausted, but I didn't want to sleep. My eyes drifted to Ramona, who was still milling through the crowd. The sun started to peek through the dark clouds, and the sound of awkward clapping at the cemetery gate caught our attention. A family of tourists stood there gawking, their cameras aloft. They had no idea that they'd just witnessed an actual vampire staking by townies.

"We're just rehearsing for the Halloween Festival," Billy Bacchus called to them with a wave. "It's going to be a real show. Make sure to get your tickets!"

A few of them waved back and began to move along.

"I'll make sure Harlow slips them some forgetting potion in their morning coffees," Jordyn whispered to me.

"Good plan," I murmured back.

29
RAMONA

Iris sat on the low wall that ran along the perimeter of the cemetery as everyone started to amble back into town. Willow had promised everyone a celebratory coffee and pastry at Witch's Brew. Nothing like slaying your enemies to bring a town together . . . and work up a wicked appetite.

The last of the townspeople soon filtered away, leaving just Iris and me. She had sticks and leaves nesting in her tousled hair and dirt on her clothes, but otherwise, she was unharmed. The shame that I had put her in danger hadn't left me just yet, but knowing that everyone had made it out alive—aside from Esme—was helping lift the weight on my chest. And judging by the expression on the witch's face, I had a feeling she'd thoroughly enjoyed being bait.

Still, no matter how much she deserved it, I couldn't believe Esme was really gone. I suspected it was loneliness that had driven her to such madness and for that, I couldn't entirely hate her, no matter how much she deserved her end. Death was no stranger to me, but even so, there were

memories Esme and I shared that would be hard to let go of. There was one thing that was for certain though: her return made me even more grateful for the people in my life.

With that thought, I perched on the cool stone next to Iris and took her hand in mine as if I did it all the time. Iris smiled before looking in the direction where Esme turned to dust.

"Well," I said wistfully, "I didn't have Randy using his own head as a weapon on this year's bingo card, but here we are." I brought the back of her hand to my lips and laid a quick kiss on her dirt-stained skin.

She chuckled. "I feel like he had been waiting a long time to do that. And staking a vampire with a broom is definitely a new one for the coven. That'll teach Agnes not to tease us at the next town meeting."

It had been quite the sight. Not that I thought the vampires would ever truly stop antagonizing the witch coven. Town traditions were important, after all.

"I'm sorry I brought all of this on you," I managed to say.

"Don't be." Iris squeezed my hand. "It was fun to have a little excitement."

I let out a contemplative hum. There was so much more I needed to say, but vulnerability was still an entirely new concept for me, and something inside of me—the cowardly part—screamed at me to give her a way out. I'd declared my affection for her to the entire town, and now, in the quiet aftermath, I was beginning to wonder if I'd taken everything too far. After all, the time Iris and I had spent together had been forced upon us. Maybe without the rush of adrenaline, things would seem different in the light of day. And while I didn't think I could survive without Iris in my arms every night, I wanted her to make the choice for herself—no strings, curses, or rogue vampires attached.

"Things can go back to the way they were now," I murmured. "You're free. No more Sherlock and Watson needed." I felt Iris's eyes on me even though I didn't look up from where our hands joined.

"Is that . . . what you want?"

"No," I admitted instantly.

A small smile tipped her lips. "Me either."

Something warm bloomed in my belly at that. "Can I say something that might be a little . . . much?"

"Is it that you want to start up our own detective agency? Because I do have a real job, actually."

"No, not that."

"Okay, then what?"

I took a deep breath, steeling myself. "You terrify me. Or rather, the way you make me feel terrifies me. I know demons don't do happily-ever-afters. I'd resigned myself to the fact that women want to be in my bed and nothing more. I was okay with it. Being unloveable—"

"You aren't unlovable," Iris cut in. "Far, far from it." She hopped up from her perch and moved to stand between my legs, draping her arms around my shoulders. "You won't judge me for admitting the way you make me feel terrifies me too?" she whispered, her eyes searching mine with all the vulnerability I couldn't show. She let out a soft laugh. "Look at us, both terrified we feel more for the other, that the feelings won't be returned, that we'll end up hurting each other . . ."

"At least we're not alone in that," I murmured, sweeping a hand down to the small of her back and gathering her closer. "I just know that if you and I take one more step forward, it will change everything within me forever."

"I think you're worth risking my heart for," Iris whispered, and my throat constricted with emotion. "I think—I *know*," she corrected, "that you're worth it."

"I love you." My lips clamped together the second the words left them. I left that proclamation just hanging there between us.

I couldn't believe I'd done it.

I'd said it aloud.

Holy shit.

I felt like I was going to throw up.

But her hands cupped my cheeks, and she pulled me into a kiss, murmuring against my mouth, "I love you too."

Disbelief coursed through me. I didn't think I'd ever be worthy of someone like her, but I couldn't deny the look in her eyes—the truth in them. She loved me. She loved me just as I loved her.

"I think I'd like to be changed forever by you too," I whispered, and her eyes misted with tears that matched my own. I dipped a finger into the collar of her sweater. "So, I guess there's only one last thing to deal with."

"How to incorporate this little vampire-staking sketch into the Halloween Festival?"

"Huh?"

"Never mind." She snickered. "What else do we have to contend with?"

"Our deal. You still owe me a proper date."

"We carved pumpkins. We spent the night together. We just trapped and killed a vampire with the entire town." She swept a hand toward the graveyard. "That didn't qualify as a date?"

"Nope." I let out a throaty chuckle. "I want you to be very sure that this is what you want before we go on our first official date."

"I do," she said instantly, and that glowing, golden warmth coursed through my veins again.

"You better be sure," I insisted.

Her lips curved. "Why?"

"Because when I call in our deal, love, I'm never letting you go."

30
IRIS

Nothing epitomized Maple Hollow quite like the night of the Halloween Festival. It was the crowning jewel of our spooky little town. Harlow, Jordyn, and I walked together through the labyrinth of stalls and lines to the middle of the candlelit square.

I felt like a giddy child. It was basically like Christmas for us witches, and I'd been delighted when the coven elders had offered to man the bookshop and apothecary tables so that Jordyn and I could explore and enjoy ourselves.

Booths had been set up in the town square throughout the week. There were stalls where you could bob for apples or participate in a pie-eating contest. There were fortunetellers and booths for cauldron elixirs. There were crafting stations where tourists could decorate their own witch hats and dip their own candles. There was even a carousel. All the youngest witches and werewolves were in line for it. Instead of horses, they would ride magically floating skeletons, pumpkins, and witches' brooms.

My favorite area was the Snack-o'-Lantern Strip that

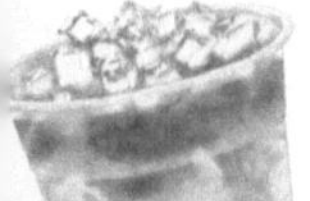

featured far more than just bowls of candy for trick-or-treaters. It had the most sinfully decadent fare the festival had to offer: candy apple bars, monster macarons, and pumpkin-spice funnel cakes.

"Willow and Wyatt's booth looks so cute." I pointed down the row to where Willow was pre-pouring cinnamon-spiced hot chocolate into cups and setting them next to the green and purple monster macarons that Wyatt had made especially for the festival.

When we got closer, Eloise spotted us. "There you are! I've been wondering when you'd show up." She looked over her shoulder then down the row as if she were about to open her jacket and reveal a bunch of counterfeit watches. But what she took out and slid across the table was far more coveted in these parts—a white pastry box. "This is the last box. You didn't get them from me."

Lightning fast, Harlow snatched it and opened the lid. "The last three apple cider donuts!" She held a hand to her chest as if deeply moved. "Thank you for saving them for us."

Jordyn plucked out a donut. "These are harder to get than drugs in this town." She made a delicious *hmm* sound when she bit into it.

I laughed as Jordyn stuffed her entire donut into her mouth. "Considering we are the only drugstore," I said, "that doesn't mean much."

"Nothing illegal in our shop!" she loudly assured everyone around us. "Only medicine."

"Thanks, Eloise." I removed a small baggie from my purse and slid it back across the table toward her. "For you. A sample of our very legal drugs."

I had put together a tea blend for uplifting and luck and

was passing it around to our closest friends. A little magic for the locals after the long—and sometimes grueling—tourist season. After tomorrow, the town would return to its normal pace, and we'd all have a chance to recover over winter.

Eloise closed her eyes and sniffed the bag. "Hmm . . . lemon balm, valerian root, and something sweet . . ."

"They're special dried blackberries that the coven propagated," Jordyn added. "Very warming. Good for the soul."

"I can't wait to try it. Thanks." Eloise tucked away her little sachet and returned to her customers.

Wyatt and Willow stood next to each other, separated only by the small gap between their tables. Though they weren't outwardly affectionate, something had clearly changed between them. Willow had explained a few bruises and scrapes the other day to Harlow, but we still felt like there was more to it than a misunderstanding with the wolf pack. A story for another time, for sure.

"Harlow, could you take these over to the vampire booth, please?" Willow held up two trays of hot chocolate, each lid balancing a crescent pastry on top. "A little thank-you to Agnes and the knitting club for making those cute tea cozies for the pots in the café."

"That's a lot for a cup of cocoa to say," Harlow jested but took the trays anyway.

"It's not just hot chocolate," Wyatt added as he filled to-go boxes with four different pastries. "I also made new macarons—vanilla with maple cream—to go with them. See?"

He held up the nearest plate for me. They were painted to look like the moon with a small willow tree in the middle. *Nice touch.*

I popped one into my mouth and let out an indecent sound at the taste. Crisp on the outside and soft on the inside. Rich and creamy. They were perfect.

He'd also made the oversized burnt maple marshmallows that topped the luscious hot chocolate.

I gave him an approving thumbs-up. "You're right. They say a lot for small cookies."

A rush of sightseers came from behind us, and we knew it was time to move on. Jordyn linked her arm with mine and we made our way through the crowd.

I panned the rest of the aisle, and my gaze finally landed on the person I'd been waiting to see. I couldn't stop the butterflies in my stomach just from seeing her. Ramona stood with Naphula on the outer edge of the square as they watched the mortals enjoy the Halloween Festival that they had likely seen a hundred times before. The two of us had agreed we'd enjoy the festivities with our best friends, each of us celebrating in kind—me with wide-eyed exuberance and Ramona with aloof wickedness.

"Are you meeting up with Ramona later?" Jordyn asked, catching my wandering eye.

"Maybe." I nudged her playfully with my elbow. "But tonight, I want to spend time with you and our friends."

She squeezed my arm, emotions cascading across her face. "Have I told you that I'm sorry for disappearing so much in the last year?"

"Yes, but you don't need to. You know I love seeing you happy." I pulled her tight to my side to avoid a group of passing teens. "I also love seeing *you*. And I know I'll be getting plenty more of that when Harlow moves in."

"Really?" She sounded surprised, but we both knew Harlow's move was long overdue. There was only so long the human could live in Willow's kitchen-stock-room-slash-guest-bedroom. And while I knew Jordyn wasn't ready for the conversation, I had a feeling a certain demon was determined that I'd never leave her bedroom again. Drawers had been cleared, favorite snacks acquired. Logically, I knew it was far too soon for any sane couple to be moving in together, but where was the sanity between witches and demons?

"So you're willing to share the bathroom with one more person?" Jordyn asked incredulously.

"If she promises to help cook every once in a while, I don't mind at all."

"Deal."

We passed the Stars and Stones booth to find Citrine directing customers toward the people helping bag orders. At first glance, I could only see my little sister, Sabine, and her girlfriend, Gwen, who'd returned from the big city this morning for the festival, but then a tall figure stood to their full height. There was only one person who could claim such a towering stature: Dean.

"Is that the new Midnight Market clerk?" Jordyn murmured, leading us closer.

The monster looked up and waved in greeting. "Iris, right?"

"Hello again, Dean." I gave an awkward half wave then turned to Citrine. "Well, you have quite the gaggle of helpers this year."

Jordyn subtly toed me with her boot, already knowing my matchmaking plans before they had even hatched.

Citrine's gaze pinged from me to Dean, her cheeks flushing.

"I'm just here for fun." Dean's chest puffed up like the

giant green Boy Scout he was. "Randy should be riding through soon, too. We have a big production to put on, you know."

Jordyn balked. "Oh yeah, we know."

The new performance had been thrown together within a couple of hours. It would be a shoddy production, but having a headless horseman in town was enough to send all the tourists into fits of applause. The trial run yesterday had people raving, which was probably why the festival was hosting its biggest crowd in decades.

"He's going to kidnap Citrine," Dean whispered conspiratorially to us.

Citrine's face turned beet red. "It's just for fun," she clarified as if it needed to be.

"Who wouldn't want to be kidnapped by Randy?" I asked, and Jordyn kicked me again. "Ouch."

"Well, we can't wait to see it!" Jordyn said, steering me away. "Have fun, all."

We linked arms and we made our way toward the vampires' game booth, where they were playing bloody beer pong.

Not their tidiest idea, but they were certainly drawing a crowd.

There, we found Harlow, who was splattered with red food coloring—I hoped. Avery stood close by, handing her sticky red ping-pong ball every time one hit the rim of a cup and bounced off.

"This is harder with thick liquid," Harlow protested. "It changes the spin on the ball."

"That's the point," Agnes griped. "If it were easy, then everyone would win a stuffed headless animal."

"All of them are handmade," Avery added. She pointed

to the knitted animals hanging above our heads—bats, cats, a raccoon even—all of them without heads.

"We had to make it hard or we'd be out before the ghoulish choir even sang."

Harlow aimed her last ball, her tongue sticking out in concentration. She launched it, but the throw was too hard and the ball went flying over the last cup. But right before it hit the ground, I gave it a little flick of my magic and guided it into one of the cups with the gelatinous mixture.

"Cheating witches," Agnes grumbled but handed Harlow a headless black moth with red and grey markings. "You better tell people where you got this."

Harlow laughed and handed the stuffed animal to Jordyn. "For you, my love."

"Aww, be still my heart." Jordyn hugged it tight and gave Harlow a sweet kiss before we continued on through the festival.

I was enjoying every bit of the magic, both real and orchestrated, but despite promising myself that I wouldn't, my eyes kept searching the darkened corners of the fair for someone, wondering if she was breaking her own promises and searching for me too.

31
RAMONA

Naphula and I wandered the edges of the Halloween Festival, liberally poured libations in hand while we surveyed the festivities from a distance like we did every year. The merriment was the perfect place for scouting future marks. Even during their happiest moments, it was easy to see the greedy and desperate ones. I had a feeling the bounty would be plentiful this year.

As we rounded the funnel cake cart, though, Naphula slowed and drew into the shadow of the nearest tree. She'd been sluggish since the curse had been lifted, but that was to be expected. The fact that she'd survived it at all was a testament to her incredible strength. The look on her face said it was more than that, though. I followed her gaze across the bustling town square to where it landed on a woman with curly blonde hair styled into a short-shaved undercut.

"Why don't you just go talk to her?" I asked, tipping my head toward Eloise, who laughed uproariously as she shared an orange popcorn ball with Willow. "I'd say she won't bite, but we both know you'd love that."

Naphula let out a long breath and shook her head, her silver hair dusting across her shoulders. "I wanted to tell you . . ." She took a long sip of her gin and tonic. "I'm heading back to London for a while. I've got a friend out there who could use a helping hand with her damned souls, and I offered to assist."

I let out a derisive huff. "So you're running away."

"Don't be so sentimental," Naphula admonished. "I need a break from the watchful eyes of little towns, from places where everyone knows each other's business. The big city will be good for me."

"This town has an attention span of two weeks, you know that," I countered. "No one will remember what happened with Esme by Christmas."

But we both knew that wasn't the reason.

"I need to clear my head," Naphula finally confessed. "My indiscretions almost cost lives."

Without even turning to look at my friend, I knew she was watching Eloise. "You should at least go say goodbye."

She shook her head. "Just add it to the list of things I've royally fucked up."

"Come on. Don't disappear into the night."

"Don't worry about it, Mona. She won't even notice I'm gone." She sounded so defeated.

"If I can manage to win the heart of a witch, you can shag a werewolf," I encouraged, my eyes searching the crowd for said witch. "You could at least—"

"Stop. Please." Naphula folded one arm across her chest, propping up her elbow to cradle her drink next to her lips.

"I've made up my mind. I'm leaving tonight. She's better off with me gone. You all are."

Stubborn. Foolish.

But all I could do was shake my head and resign myself to enjoying the last bit of time with my friend before she left on a new adventure.

"Do you need me to water your plants?" I asked into my drink.

"It'll be easier if you take them off my hands until I get back in the spring."

"Six months?" I balked. "You must be down worse than I thought."

"Six months is minutes for us," she said. "Besides, I really don't want to hang around for the disgusting love fest I know is about to take place between you and that little redhead."

My eyes found Iris across the crowd, as if just thinking about her had summoned her from the fray. She was in a circle with Jordyn, Harlow, Willow, and Wyatt, throwing her head back and laughing with her whole body. I knew the exact sound she was making without even hearing it. My lips curled up despite themselves.

"Point made." I playfully punched Naphula's arm. "I'm still going to miss you."

"Thank you for not hating me," she replied, and I was struck by the sadness in her voice. "I'm sorry—"

"I am as petty and vengeful as they come, Naph. But there are no grudges between us," I assured her. "I'm more upset that you didn't think you could talk to me than anything else."

"I know."

I wrapped an arm around her shoulders and pulled her in for a rare show of affection. "I forgive you."

"Thank you."

Just as quickly as the hug started, we pulled apart. Thirty seconds was the maximum amount of affection time two demons could share.

"Just promise you'll come home," I continued with a gentle laugh. "There are good things waiting for you here."

She shook her head again. "Not all of us are as brave as you, Ramona." She swigged back the rest of her drink. "I'd rather face the fires of hell than a wolf girl with my heart on a leash. Nothing a six-month romp around London won't fix. Just as it always does."

I pursed my lips, knowing my friend was a fool but accepting there was nothing I could do about it.

"I'm going to have my work cut out for me being the only demon in town," I said with a dramatic sigh while I directed us to a rather sour-looking man who was lurking near the pumpkin-carving station. "Come on. Let's go make a few more deals before you go."

We walked through the chilled air and descended on the unsuspecting out-of-towners until our metaphorical pockets were full of new deals. I found my cash cow in a group of businessmen who were all looking to be promoted over each other. Like fish in a barrel. Naphula, on the other hand, was feeling most generous and promised fame and riches to several social media influencers who were in town chasing their next viral video.

When she closed her last deal, she gave me a single nod, and I returned it before she disappeared into the night. Naphula and I didn't do goodbyes.

As the evening wound down, I idled in the shadows, watching Iris and her friends. The town's brand-new reenactment of defeating a *legendary* evil vampire was a hilarious shitshow, but entertaining, nevertheless. After the show, Iris and her friends continued to hop between the stalls and played games into the wee hours of the night before eventually relenting to their exhaustion and heading back to the apothecary just before dawn.

Once I knew my witch was home safe, I walked back to my house. Even though I'd just seen Iris cross the threshold of the Poison Apple, when I saw a figure standing outside my door, I thought it was her. Instead, it was someone I hadn't expected at all.

"Agnes," I said as I approached the gate. "I refuse to be part of that ridiculous play next year. I don't care that I have the perfect—What's wrong?"

The deep-set wrinkle on her brow drew tighter than usual. "We found out who taught Esme that dark magic." She stood as still as death. "It was another demon who taught her the curse."

"Who?"

"They were exorcised years ago and bound to hell. At least . . . that was until Esme broke them out. We have it on good authority that he's looking for a new place to move. A paranormal paradise."

"Fuck," I grumbled. "Where are they now?"

"They've petitioned the town council to take up residence here. Claiming sanctuary."

"And what does the town council think about that?" I asked tightly.

She held out a sealed letter in response. The dark red, stamped wax seal told me all I needed to know.

Lucifer.

This fucking demon had made an official request not just with the town council, but with hell itself.

I took the letter from Agnes's outstretched hand. As soon as it touched my skin, it opened on its own, floating just in front of my face for me to read. Each line of the text disappeared the second after I read it:

———

My most vicious Ramona,

You are hereby requested to attend the hearing of King of Hell, Zagan. Your expert testimony is required on the petition of residency in regard to your mortal domain. Upon the rules of the plane, you must appear in situ to contest or approve such a request. Your presence is expected immediately and without convenience.

Wicked regards,
Lucifer, Emperor

———

Shit.

As the letter disintegrated into embers, I felt the pull from beyond the veil starting to take hold like a lasso around my middle.

With a grumble, I straightened my cufflinks, glad I'd decided on Cartier earlier today as it seemed I would be making an impromptu appearance in hell. "Agnes, tell Iris I'll be back as soon as I can."

"Will do." Agnes nodded. "Where should I tell her you've gone?"

I rolled my eyes. "Demonic jury duty." And then I was taken into the void, the vampire's pitying cackle following me.

32
IRIS

It had been two weeks since Ramona had been called away. The longest two weeks of my life. When she'd left, everything between us had been so new, and with every passing day, little fissures of doubt crept in. Would she be the same when she returned? Would she still feel the same way about me?

The only thing that kept me from spiraling out was helping Jordyn. If it hadn't been for her planning on proposing to Harlow, I would've spent all day rereading the brimstone-scented letters that appeared on my pillow each morning.

It felt like just yesterday when the café owner's little sister had stumbled into our apothecary. I couldn't believe a whole year had passed since I'd first seen that glimmer in Jordyn's eye, like a veil being lifted away to reveal her brightness underneath. I had Harlow to thank for bringing out the best in her, for being not only an amazing partner to Jordyn, but a caring friend to me.

I felt the threads of time weaving around the frozen air

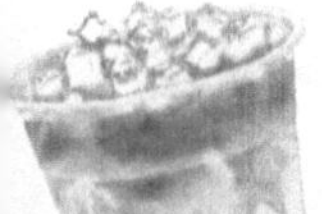

as Jordyn and I stood in the gazebo, bathed in a halo of flickering candlelight.

Candles that had taken several hours to perfectly arrange and light, thank you and you're welcome.

Memories of our friendship were everywhere. Chasing each other through the square as witchlings, our first crushes, carrying our crafts-laden backpacks home from witch summer camp, getting drunk on our first bottle of witch wine and doing a terrible job convincing the coven we were sober.

A lot of life had happened within this town square. And now, just like the moon we prayed to, the day had come when Jordyn was about to move into a new phase: fiancée, then wife.

Well, if Harlow said yes, of course.

"You're going to wear a hole in the floor doing that," I chastised, watching Jordyn make yet another short circuit across the well-worn planks. "Calm down before Billy makes us repaint it."

"I can't calm down." She checked her watch. Again. "They should be here by now. Willow said three. Willow's never late."

"Yeah, but Harlow is. She probably just wanted to stay longer," I tried to reassure her. "And Willow didn't have a good enough excuse for getting her back here without telling her why. Everything is fine. Everything is going to plan." The tension on Jordyn's face eased only slightly.

I'd been training for this moment—calming down my best friend on the precipice of her engagement—my whole life.

"I'm freezing my ass off here." Agnes's shrill voice came from behind one of the bare maples just off the path.

"You all don't need to be here!" Jordyn shouted back loud enough to remind everyone within earshot. "Why don't you all just go home?"

"And miss this?" Rudy called from behind the shabby black rose bush, the last leaves clinging to its spindly orb. "Our Jordyn's getting married. Besides, it's not *that* cold."

"Easy for you to say," Agnes threw back. "You don't even have an ass."

I stifled a giggle as a smattering of snickers rang out from all the different hiding spots. Randy and Dean had helped Rudy and I set up all the candles so they were—in theory—here for a reason. But the rest of the town had snuck into their positions once Jordyn and I had finished placing everything just so. A lit-up witch-hat gazebo was Maple Hollow's Bat-Signal. Everyone came out of the woodwork when it was on.

"They're going to ruin this for me, aren't they?" Jordyn worried her lip, looking like she would burst into tears at any moment.

"It's going to be fine," I said in my most soothing tone. Lucky for us, I had just the thing to help ease the tension. "Do you want something for the nerves?"

She narrowed her eyes. "Why are you so chill?"

"I may have smoked some calming herbs before we came out here." I snorted with laughter. "It's a new blend. We're going to be rich as thieves."

"I thought I told you no dipping into the apothecary stash." She pointed an accusatory finger at me. "And if you do, you have to share with me."

Jordyn held out a hand, and I rummaged through my pockets, only to realize that I may have used up the last of what I'd brought while setting out the candles. To be fair, it had taken over an hour. Those wobbly bastards wouldn't stay put—even with magic—and I'd lost track of myself with the repetitive motions.

"Sorry!" I pulled out the insides of my empty pockets. "Next time!"

Next time? As if she were going to get engaged again.

Jordyn rolled her eyes, but I knew she'd want to be mentally present for one of the most important moments of her life. Just then, Dougall came running down the road, his arms windmilling when he hit a patch of black ice. "Their car is just turning off Misty Lane! I repeat, their car is turning off Misty Lane! Less than ten minutes to go, people!"

With that, he fell into a pile of snow, eliciting a hushed gasp from the crowd surrounding us.

"And that's our chief of police, ladies, gentlemen, fangs, and ghouls," Jordyn muttered under her breath.

Dougall scrambled to his feet and dusted the snow off his uniform, then ducked behind the steps of the gazebo, not at all conspicuous. Everyone had the best intentions, but I could tell Jordyn was worried that someone would pipe up during her and Harlow's big moment.

Which was why I had a little trick up my sleeve.

When Willow's car came into view, I readied my magic, gathering it in my fingertips and reciting the silencing spell in my mind. Taking in a deep breath, I opened my mouth, only to be stopped by the sound of someone clearing their throat behind us. My teeth snapped shut. Then Jordyn and I whirled around, only to find none other than Ramona standing there, her hands clasped in front of her like a bouncer. She wore a spotless black trench coat over her regular uniform of a well-tailored suit.

My heart skipped several beats.

She was here. She was back.

All my excitement deflated as quickly as it had burst to life.

Why did it have to be now? Why did it have to be when I couldn't jump into her arms and never let go?

"Ramona," I whispered, but it came out more like a scold, "if you're going to be here, you need to hide."

"I've come to collect on a debt," she said with a menacing smile. "Time's up, witchling."

"What are you talking about?" I hissed.

"You agreed to a date." Ramona's feral grin was tinged with a darker menace that only hell could bring forth. "Within a year. And I have given you much longer than that out of the sheer kindness of my heart."

My whole body vibrated at the rough rasp of her words. She was so still, so cold, but her eyes burned with an unspoken need.

"Can this please wait a couple minutes? Please?"

"I am good at many things. Waiting isn't one of them."

"You can wait just a tiny bit longer," I pushed.

"Give me a time and I'll go."

She was in her true demonic element, and I knew I was in for it. "This is ridiculous," I complained, knowing Willow's car would turn around the bend at any moment.

"I can hear the car!" Dougall called from his hiding spot.

"Iris," Jordyn whined and flashed me a pleading look.

"You have to go," I ordered Ramona. We could hash this out after my best friend's engagement.

I placed my hands on Ramona's hips. The weak attempt to push her away was more of an excuse to be close to her, even for a few seconds, but she didn't so much as budge.

"Goddess, are you made of stone?"

"Iris!" Jordyn snapped, doubling the pace of her nervous bouncing. "This is kind of important. Just pick a time!"

"Okay, fine!" I said, exasperated. "You can pick me up at seven. We'll go eat at the new Italian place."

Ramona gave me a wink. *Goddess, I missed that wink.* "Done." She lowered her mouth to the shell of my ear and whispered, "Wear the sweater I made for you," before disappearing into thin air.

"Delightful. A date with a demon." Jordyn shook her head teasingly. "What are your parents going to say? What is the coven going to say? Also, that's one hell of an age gap between you two—"

My elbow met her ribs right as a car pulled into the square. "Worry about that later," I said, then dashed down the steps to hide behind the nearest bush, nearly falling face-first into a crusty pile of snow.

The last rustling noises and whispers were met with one last chorus of, "Shush!" before Willow's car slowed to a halt and Harlow stepped out of it.

It was actually happening.

Harlow was getting out of the car. My best friend was finally getting her happily-ever-after. And later tonight, come hell or high water, I was determined to get mine.

33
RAMONA

Demons *aren't supposed to get butterflies in their stomachs*, I told myself as I strode up to Iris's apartment door three minutes to seven. One of many rules I seemed to be breaking of late. I'd been summoned to hell only a couple of days ago in my own mind, but time worked differently on that plane. It had been weeks for Iris, and I hoped nothing had changed between us while I'd been away. Given the playful welcome I'd gotten a few hours before, I had high hopes. But hope had always been my Achilles' heel.

Nerves coiled tighter in my stomach.

Get your shit together, Ramona. It's just a date.

But I knew in truth, it was much, much more.

Lifting my hand to knock, I barely touched the wood before it flew open and an unimpressed Jordyn was standing in the doorway.

The near-smile I wore instantly evaporated.

"I'm here for Iris," I said, panning over her crossed arms to the ring on her finger. "Congrats, by the way."

"I thought you and I should have a quick talk before you take Iris out." Jordyn took a step out onto the doormat and shut the door behind her. "I know this date is supposed to close out your deal, but if you disappear afterward and leave my best friend heartbroken, I will hunt you down and exorcize the shit out of you. Got it?"

Sparks shot out of her fingertips in warning. Whether for effect or out of anger, I didn't care to be threatened. "If this is your version of the intentions talk, I'd like to remind you that I am a demon."

"I know that," she snapped. "But you also needed the reminder about who you'll have to deal with if you hurt Iris. And the line starts with me." She leaned in. "And it's a long fucking line in this town."

Iris was just as loved as I was by the residents of Maple Hollow, and a relationship in a small town never ended with just the two people involved in it. A falling out between us would probably result in the fracturing of town lines. That thought had already crossed my mind. Would they divide the town up into quadrants if something happened between us? Would people would wear devil horns or witch hat pins in shows of solidarity? Seven Hells, I wouldn't put it past them.

I squared the witch with a look. "Never going to happen. You have my word."

"Good." She reached a hand over her shoulder and knocked twice on the door. "Welcome home, by the way."

The door opened and Iris stepped out next to her friend. She looked stunning in the sweater I'd knitted for her, a long black skirt with a slit up to her thigh, and a pair of high-heeled black boots. My jaw dropped. How she effortlessly went from adorable apothecary witch to devastatingly sexy vixen with just some lipstick, mascara, and an up-do was pure magic.

She smiled.

I melted.

"Ready to go?" I asked.

"Have her home by tomorrow night," Jordyn told me while giving her friend a hug. "We have an engagement party to plan."

I rolled my eyes but returned Iris's smile. "Aye, aye, captain."

Iris took my hand, and we heard Jordyn call down the stairs, "Have fun, love bats!"

In a quick ten-minute walk, we reached Trattoria Occulto. The owners, part of the local nymph community, knew I had a special interest in expanding the businesses in town, so in exchange for their ongoing success, Iris and I would always have a table. It was an easy deal. No messy soul brokering this time.

"*Bella serata. Venite,*" Nerine, the owner greeted us at the door, her golden bracelets jangling as she waved us in. "*Benvenuti.* We've prepared the table you requested."

"Umm, wow." Iris looked up at me. "Did you bribe them or something? I feel like I'm in a mafia novel."

My brow rose. "You think the nymphs aren't in the mafia?"

Nerine leaned in and whispered conspiratorially, "*Autentica.*"

She led us to the farthest corner booth, where two candles sat with a small bouquet of black roses in between. The decor was a mixture of Roman Gothic and Sicilian art. Some pieces I'd personally donated from my own collection. Beautiful stained-glass windows with images of men's heads on golden platers gave the space a spooky but, in my opinion, elegant feel.

Every table was occupied and there was a line out the door. These nymphs had been perfecting their recipes since the days of Ancient Rome, and since they'd broken ground on the establishment last year, I'd known the restaurant would become an instant Maple Hollow favorite.

"Here are your menus, but we also have a tasting *prix fixe* that everyone is raving about." Nerine waited for us to take our seats then offered us two sheets. "Here is the wine list. The pairings were chosen specifically for the chef's menu."

"You really outdid yourselves." Iris beamed up at Nerine. The nymph's ethereal eyes shimmered with pride. "Maple Hollow has never had a restaurant like this before. It's gorgeous."

"*Grazie, tesoro.*" Nerine snapped her fingers, and ice water filled our glasses magically as she walked away, leaving us marveling.

"I heard Trattoria Occulta was going to be the talk of the town, but this is next level." Iris picked up her water and took a sip then focused on me. "Tell me about hell. Other than what you said in your letters."

"Those were hardly letters. I didn't even get to tell you about all the wicked things I was imagining about you during those long hours in court."

She planted her arm on the table to prop up her chin. "Okay, forget hell. Tell me about that instead."

"How about I show you later?" I offered, reaching into my pocket and taking out the gift I'd brought for her.

Nerves ignited anew as I slid the rectangular, red velvet box across the table.

Iris's eyes went wide. "What is this?" She didn't wait for an answer before opening it with a squeal. "It's beautiful!"

The necklace was made of hellfire-forged gold with a flame queen opal. The flashes of reds, purples, and blues sparkled when she held it up to the candlelight.

"I have something for you, too." She practically vibrated with excitement as she dug into her tote bag and pulled out a brown paper package. "I had Jordyn wrap it, but I poured the seal."

I eyed the wax seal over a sprig of lavender. It was my sigil. She'd crafted it perfectly and in doing so made me feel more acknowledged than if she'd used my title or name.

This present was for *me* in all that I was.

I carefully opened the package around the seal, intending to keep it, as I racked my brain as to what she had thought I, of all people, needed. After centuries of collecting and curating, there was nothing, aside from her in my bed. But the moment I lifted the box's lid, I knew I was wrong. Inside was a set of beautiful stained-wood knitting needles, a protection spell carved in scrawling Latin up the sides. And inlaid in silver at the tops were iris flowers.

Tears pricked my eyes. I'd never felt more deeply seen. The gift left me speechless.

"Do you like them? I carved and stained them myself. Though, I did get the wood from Wyatt. He's been spending a lot of time camping lately and brought back a branch from one of the oldest oak trees in the haunted wood for me, and—"

I was on my feet and over to her side of the booth before she could even finish her sentence. I pulled Iris into me, pressing my lips to hers. She was stunned for a moment, and she wrapped her arms around me, a hand gripping the back of my neck to deepen the long overdue kiss.

"I'll take that as approval," she whispered against my mouth. "I really missed you."

"I more than missed you," I said, the knots in my stomach tightening.

All the plans in my mind unfurled, my lips on hers a silent promise that I'd be everything she needed and so much more.

My little witch.

My heart—one I thought would never be so full.

I was beginning to realize that there was more magic in Maple Hollow than just spells and curses. Something that felt a lot more like fate. No deal or scheme would ever feel as satisfying—as perfectly *right*—as Iris's hand in mine.

"What are you thinking about?" Iris asked with a knowing smile as I brushed my lips across hers again.

The last vestiges of my control were about to snap, and I was going to splay her across this table of expensive pasta and take her.

I cleared my throat. "Nothing."

"I've been thinking about nothing a lot too," she said, her fingers pressing tighter into my clothes.

Seven Hells. If we made it through the first course, it would be a miracle.

"So I guess this date concludes our deal," Iris said, dousing ice on my libido. My gut clenched as her hand mindlessly drifted to her collarbone.

I swallowed thickly. "I suppose it does."

When I'd called in our deal, I'd told her I was never letting her go. I'd told her I loved her, and she'd told me she loved me in return.

But what if something had changed in the time I'd been gone? Was love not enough? Was this it?

Fear climbed up my throat.

It couldn't be . . .

Iris took my hands in hers and squeezed, making me meet her gaze. "So I'd like to propose another deal. A trade, really."

"Oh?" I tried to sound calm even as fear roiled like a storm in my chest.

A soft, nervous smile flickered across her lips. "My heart," she whispered. "Forever. In exchange for yours."

Tears welled in my eyes, my hands squeezing hers tighter and tighter as emotions choked my throat. I looked at her with all the promise and reverence she deserved. Her magic was the only kind I'd ever need.

"It's a deal."

Want to read Iris and Ramona's second kiss??

Check out our witchy summer camp side quest, *Cauldrons & Campfires.* (This story takes place between the events of *Pumpkin Spice & Poltergeist* and *Curses & Cold Brew!*)

ACKNOWLEDGMENTS

This book couldn't have happened without Caroline Acebo, Norma Gambini, and Holly Dunn. What a dream this process has been!

Thank you to all of our Patreon members who support our dreams, art addictions, mini series and bonus stories. Your support means the world to us!